"I told you long ago that we would remain married only as long as necessary," Tadeo told her, no longer caring how dark he sounded.

It needed to be done. It didn't matter *how* it was done. "I've come here to let you know that I intend to begin our divorce proceedings. Immediately."

Tadeo didn't know what he expected.

But of all the possible responses he'd imagined, it wasn't the way she smiled at him.

Her lips curved gently. Even kindly, he thought.

And then she rose.

The fabric cascaded off her and slid in heaps of shimmering color to either side of her, landing on the tiles at her feet.

It was impossible. It was inconceivable.

It was a disaster of epic proportions and she was *smiling*—

"About that divorce," Esme said, as if they were discussing the weather. Or what to have the staff prepare for a snack. As if she was not very obviously *pregnant*. "I wonder if you might want to rethink it."

USA TODAY bestselling, RITA® Award–nominated and critically acclaimed author **Caitlin Crews** has written more than one hundred and thirty books and counting. She has a master's and PhD in English literature, thinks everyone should read more category romance and is always available to discuss her beloved alpha heroes—just ask. She lives in the Pacific Northwest with her comic book–artist husband, is always planning her next trip and will never, ever read all the books in her to-be-read pile. Thank goodness.

Books by Caitlin Crews

Harlequin Presents

Forbidden Royal Vows
Greek's Christmas Heir
Her Accidental Spanish Heir
Forbidden Greek Mistress
An Heir for Christmas
Sicilian Devil's Prisoner

The Diamond Club

Pregnant Princess Bride

Notorious Mediterranean Marriages

Greek's Enemy Bride
Carrying a Sicilian Secret

Work Wives to Billionaires' Wives

Kidnapped for His Revenge

Visit the Author Profile page
at Harlequin.com for more titles.

KING'S HEIR OF HATE

CAITLIN CREWS

PRESENTS

If you purchased this book without a cover you should be aware that this book is stolen property. It was reported as "unsold and destroyed" to the publisher, and neither the author nor the publisher has received any payment for this "stripped book."

Recycling programs for this product may not exist in your area.

ISBN-13: 978-1-335-21358-7

King's Heir of Hate

Copyright © 2026 by Caitlin Crews

All rights reserved. No part of this book may be used or reproduced in any manner whatsoever without written permission.

Without limiting the exclusive rights of any author, contributor or the publisher of this publication, any unauthorized use of this publication to train generative artificial intelligence (AI) technologies is expressly prohibited. Harlequin also exercises their rights under Article 4(3) of the Digital Single Market Directive 2019/790 and expressly reserves this publication from the text and data mining exception.

This is a work of fiction. Names, characters, places and incidents are either the product of the author's imagination or are used fictitiously. Any resemblance to actual persons, living or dead, businesses, companies, events or locales is entirely coincidental.

For questions and comments about the quality of this book, please contact us at CustomerService@Harlequin.com.

TM and ® are trademarks of Harlequin Enterprises ULC.

Harlequin Enterprises ULC
22 Adelaide St. West, 41st Floor
Toronto, Ontario M5H 4E3, Canada
www.Harlequin.com

HarperCollins Publishers
Macken House, 39/40 Mayor Street Upper,
Dublin 1, D01 C9W8, Ireland
www.HarperCollins.com

Printed in Lithuania

KING'S HEIR OF HATE

CHAPTER ONE

His Majesty Xavier Tadeo Santiago did not have to make it all the way up the drive to the remote manor house in the farthest reaches of the royal estate to know that it was far past time to divorce his queen.

The drive itself was a pageant of early spring flowers flung in all directions like a discordant quilt. They were clumped here and festooned there, their bright colors clashing with each other and running all over the place, making a dramatic visual cacophony on both sides of the drive.

He found them offensive at once.

Tadeo was well acquainted with the work of the groundskeeper and his staff. They kept the rest of the royal estate in pristine and orderly condition, as was right and proper, since the royal family served its subjects and was called to present—always—their best foot forward. These grounds belonged to the kingdom. As did the palace, its contents, and indeed, the royal family itself.

Even the king himself was no more or less than the property of the kingdom, or so Tadeo's father had always taught him.

It meant more with the ghost of Tadeo's mother hanging always between them. The spectacle she'd made of herself. The shame and scandal she'd rained down upon the palace and the kingdom. His father had done his best to remain stalwart in the face of her behavior—always an uphill battle.

Now it was Tadeo's duty to take up the mantle that his father had carried until the day of his death five months ago. It had taken him all of this time to feel comfortable in the role that he had been preparing for all his life. It had required all of his focus and commitment to make the transition from his father's reign to his own as seamless as possible. There had been the somber funeral, then the burial, then the typical period of mourning.

But spring was coming. The Kingdom of Bellaza was coming alive after its cold, hard winter.

Tadeo needed to divorce his wife and move on—though, to minimize scandal and disruption, the divorce would have to be civilized. He had already plotted out the messaging with his team, and he had come to do this unpleasant task in person because he felt that was appropriate and a husband owed a wife that much. He assumed that it would be an uncomfortable conversation, perhaps, but a brief one.

After all, he had made it perfectly clear during their widely publicized courtship that this was precisely what would happen once he became king. They would play the part of a royal couple so well-suited to each other that their subjects made up happy endings for them—though there would be precious few public displays as they went about their official duties. Tadeo's family was well known for its adherence to the strictest protocol.

They would let the public make whatever meal it liked from perfectly polite and expected touches.

Tadeo had been told there was fan fiction about their private life all over the internet. He chose not to know what that was.

But this marriage would end. They would never see each other again once they navigated their way through a divorce so amicable it would be applauded. He'd already spent time with his team plotting out the details. Once the divorce was handled, after a suitable period of reflection, Tadeo would find a far more suitable queen and set about making the heir the kingdom required.

He had spent seven years making certain that he saw Esme only when required to for the work they did, never in any private capacity that could lead to complications in his plan in the form of the child he adamantly did not want with her.

Well, a voice in him chided, *you managed it for almost all of those seven years, anyway.*

Tadeo did not wish to think about that one slip, five months ago. There were other, more pressing things at the moment, like the fact that the condition of the manor's grounds appalled him. More than that, the sight seemed to dig beneath his skin, as if she—and he knew it was her, if not with her own hands, then at her express direction—had planted all of the flowers in as unorthodox a fashion as possible *specifically* to bother him.

Queen Esme, betrothed to him since the day of her birth, his wife for the past seven years—and for one reckless year across an ocean in a foreign city, his lover—was astoundingly good at bothering him. She had a talent for getting under his skin in a way no one else could. Or ever had.

A reality that he had never come to terms with, though he had learned how to control his reactions to her over the years of their marriage. Tadeo, in truth, did not wish to come to terms with the ways Esme got to him. None of that mattered now.

"It all ends today," he assured himself, his voice a dark spool of sound in the interior of the car.

He was glad he was alone.

Tadeo had driven himself, waving off his usual guards because he did not intend to leave the royal estate. Now, still on the garish drive, he slowed the vintage Rolls-Royce that had been a part of his grandfather's collection and ordered himself to find his center. To remain calm.

Something that was normally not the least bit difficult for him.

Only Esme disrupted his equanimity. Only Esme forced him to confront the distasteful evidence that he truly was his mother's son, made of all the wild, impossible parts of her that had led her to make such a display of herself for all the world to see. He loathed that he possessed such depths inside himself and had spent most of his adult life doing all that he could to keep them locked away.

He could not be the king his country deserved unless and until he removed Esme from his life. He had known this going in, but there had always been so much investment in the fairy-tale notion of the Prince of Bellaza marrying the Princess of Clarebonne from the neighboring kingdom. Not least because the two kingdoms had been one, long ago, and this only added to the fairy-tale mystique. After the scandal his mother had wrought on her marriage and therefore also on Tadeo's father's reign, a fairy tale had seemed like a gift. A gift that could fix what his mother had broken.

But the fairy tale had run its course. Now was the time to act, and Tadeo was ready. He was more than ready.

Their marriage would end quietly. There were no children after seven years of living completely separate lives in private, so there was no claim to the throne to worry about. Esme could go off to make a mess of whatever she wished, wherever she wished to do it, without it having any bearing on him.

Just so long as she left Bellaza and Tadeo never laid eyes on her again, he would be happy.

Because he would finally be able to *breathe*.

He would not let her damned flowers get to him, reminding him of too many things he did not wish to think about. All of them involving Esme and that recklessness only she conjured up in him. He would see to it that her gardening additions were summarily removed as soon as she left the manor house and replaced with a tidy hedge. There would be no sign of Esme's disruptive presence once she left, and that was what mattered. This chapter of his life was finally ending.

And not a moment too soon.

The drive wound around at last to the house itself, which was a fine old Bellazan structure made in the late medieval period, then renovated time and again in the centuries since to suit the whims of a succession of queens. When Tadeo had handed it off to his brand-new queen on their wedding night, it had been a sturdy, quietly elegant monument of the kingdom's history. He had not been here since.

An oversight, clearly.

Tadeo was not certain that he could entirely believe his own eyes as he gazed out at the monstrosity that loomed before him at the top of the drive.

She had...painted it, if that was what it could be called. What she'd done was gaudy. It was an *assault*.

In place of the expected white walls and red-tiled rooftops that nodded toward the kingdom's Spanish neighbors, plus the hint of the nearby French countryside in the sprawling gardens that would not look out of place surrounding a chateau, the Queen's Manor House—once considered the refined jewel of the royal estate—now appeared to have been vomited upon by an intoxicated rainbow.

Tadeo was so aghast at the tasteless horror show in front of him that he almost forgot to step on the brake in the car. He rolled to a stop only centimeters from crashing into the insufferably bright magenta wall before him. He continued to stare out through the windshield, not able to accept that he was truly seeing the ornate, excessive, and expansive palate of too many colors before him.

He wondered if it was possible that he was, in fact, having a stroke.

At least that sensation was familiar.

It was much the way he had felt the morning after his father's death five months ago, when he had woken to find that it wasn't a dream. Not only was his noble and admirable father truly dead, when the old man had always seemed so invincible, but Tadeo had actually gone and done the one thing he'd vowed he would never, ever do.

He had allowed Esme into his bed. Or rather, a couch in his father's study, but it was the same regret either way.

Tadeo knew better.

God help him, did he know better.

He could recall that morning perfectly. How he had lain there on the couch in the study where she'd found him after the funeral, feeling as if he was fracturing into a thousand shards of jagged glass as she curled up at his side. She was so peaceful. She looked like an angel as she slept, the way she always had.

She still fit against his body perfectly.

It seemed impossible, after all those years, and yet there was no denying it.

Tadeo had felt as if his chest was cracked wide open, and she was to blame for it.

Just as she had been the first time, years ago, when they'd finally met each other on the other side of the world. He had been doing his graduate work in the sort of business, economics, and public policy issues that could only serve the kingdom. She had been an undergraduate in the same city. A city that seemed like a long-lost daydream to him now. The Boston of his memories was always covered in towers of snow to mark its bitter winters. There were no mountains to speak of, when Bellaza was ringed with them. More, the wild Atlantic was forever seething about at the end of streets and in the distance, as if keeping watch.

He liked to tell himself that he had been happy to leave that strange, small city—but he still woke up from dreams that smelled like the salt marshes of Cape Cod on a quiet spring morning, or sounded like the rattle of the T, or had him remembering walking along the Charles River on a picture-perfect fall afternoon.

Tadeo exited the car outside the manor house, shutting the driver's door sharply behind him. Then realized that he was standing about because he wasn't used to arriving anywhere and not being immediately greeted by staff. He was quite certain that there was staff at the manor house. What he did not understand was why none of them made themselves known as protocol demanded.

Thoughts of Boston felt like a reprimand, but then, he had known at the time that those years were an indulgence. That he was permitted to indulge in a kind of freedom there—the independence to walk where he pleased and live a life with far less scrutiny in a country not his own. He had known he never would again.

Still, he found himself shaking off unwanted memories yet again as he started for the main door, painted in a revolting shade of pink. If he was a vindictive man, he might have been tempted to make Esme pay to restore the house to its traditional state before releasing her. But that would only prolong this.

And to Tadeo's way of thinking, their entire relationship had already been entirely too prolonged.

He had known that he was betrothed since he was a child. He was five years older than Esme and had been showed pictures of her over time. She had been raised in Clarebonne, which was even smaller than Bellaza and had always enjoyed favorable relations with it, dating all the way back to the time in antiquity when the kingdoms had been joined. Their betrothal had been speculated about in the press all throughout their teenage years because it was not a formal, legal betrothal in the old style. It was an understanding.

An understanding between two kings was as good as law, in some places, but the two kings in question had been very deliberate about the way they'd handled Esme and Tadeo. The two of them had not met. They were deliberately kept apart, in fact.

No one expects you and Esme to molder on shelves, at least until you meet, Tadeo's father, King Hugo, had always said. *You can enjoy yourself as you wish, as long as you remain* ever-conscious *of your duties and* scrupulous *about your reputation.*

Yes, sir, Tadeo had murmured. He had been all of fourteen and did not wish to think about his duties any more than necessary, given he had already found them crushing. Much less his spotless reputation, though that part he was admittedly more concerned with.

King Alain and I are agreed that you and Princess Esme should meet when she is finished with her studies. What that means, his father had said, perhaps more sternly than before, *is that you may do what you wish, but you should never be linked in public with another woman. Neither one of you must ever be seen in any kind of amorous situation, or in any questionable position that could be interpreted the wrong way. You might find this onerous. But it is excellent practice for your future.* His craggy face, with the blue eyes Tadeo had inherited, had been somber. *I expect there to be no scandals, Tadeo. Not one, not ever. Do you understand?*

Tadeo had always understood.

He had only been eleven when his mother had died, off in a boating accident in Italy with one of her many lovers. Some had claimed that Tadeo was too young to understand what was happening then, but they were mistaken. He had understood completely. And even if he hadn't, he certainly would have heard every sordid detail at school, where his status as crown prince had long since lost its luster.

Even if he'd wished to avoid his mother's exploits, he'd been unable to.

For years at that point, it had been impossible for Tadeo to avoid the sordid details that his mother seemed to have no shame sharing with the whole world. Everybody knew the story of the selfish, unsatisfied Queen of Bellaza who had provided the kingdom with its needed heir and then declared her duties and responsibilities completed.

The rest of my life is mine, cries the Queen! the headlines screamed.

Tadeo had understood completely and totally that he could not, as that queen's son, create that kind of scandal. No matter what.

Even if he hadn't been told exactly that by his father, repeatedly, he would have come to the same conclusion himself. The kingdom prized its calmness. Its peace. Scandals were for other, more volatile nations.

It was Tadeo's duty not to become a scandal. He took that seriously.

He had therefore enjoyed himself, but always with women who understood his position. And who, more to the point, he trusted not to sell him out to the papers. This meant that he was significantly less of a player than many of his boarding school friends, but he would not be the one to put the family's name into the mud again.

He had vowed it after his mother's funeral. It was the first, last, and only time he had ever seen his father cry. Or, more precisely, allow his eyes to look damp. For the smallest moment.

Tadeo had learned over time that there were warning signs when a woman he might have been interested in was the wrong choice. Bright red flags that would indicate when a woman was appropriate for him or not, and it was his duty to look for those flags and react accordingly. He liked the women he dated, very privately, to be circumspect in all things. Modest, practical, and smart enough to think twice when it came to exposing him.

He had never chosen wrong.

If it had been up to him, he would never have chosen Princess Esme.

Tadeo had been the one to initiate their meeting in Boston. He'd been in graduate school across the river in Cambridge and even though he did not go out of his way to keep up with the Princess's every move, he could not avoid knowing that she was attending nearby Wellesley College, a very highly selective women's college with an august reputation.

His palace handlers—now his team—made certain he knew.

They were both far away from the intense press interest that surrounded them in their own countries. They were both still immersed in their studies, so there would be no chance of accelerating the march toward their wedding. Tadeo had thought it would be safe. Easy. A smart move to build a friendship in advance, so that the years they would spend together as husband and wife could only be better for it.

Too well had he understood the point of the stories King Hugo had told about his own courtship of Tadeo's mother. Lady Marisol had not been his family's first choice. She had not been a choice at all. She had been impetuous, bright, and bold. The King had fallen hard and had insisted that he would marry her or he would not marry at all.

But soon enough, Marisol had grown bored of royal life. Just as everyone had warned the King she would.

What had followed had haunted his father for the rest of his life, and now haunted Tadeo too. The ghost of Marisol was what lay beneath every decision and every plan Tadeo made for his life and his reign. He thought about the scenes she had made, the extramarital affairs she had flaunted, the contempt with which she had treated the kingdom in general and his father in particular, and vowed to do whatever was necessary to protect the kingdom from a repeat of such embarrassment.

He had married Esme because their kingdoms were invested in their wedding, a choice he would make again if necessary. Just as he would divorce her now because she could never be an appropriate mother to his heir. She was too difficult. Too...problematic.

Back in Boston, Tadeo had possessed absolutely no desire to repeat history. He'd had no intention of ever allowing the kind of passion that had blindsided his father and made him turn his back on his kingdom for the pleasures of the flesh to level him as well.

He had been completely and totally unprepared for Esme, in other words.

Another familiar feeling he very much wished to banish from his life entirely.

No servants appeared at the door, or responded when he knocked, so he opened it himself and went inside. And in case he'd imagined that the exterior of the building was the only place that his wife had allowed her creativity free reign, he was quickly disabused of that notion.

The color scheme—though that word, *scheme*, suggested some kind of a plan, which Tadeo doubted very much had been used here—continued inside. He walked through, finding that his jaw was tense and that he was grinding his teeth as he looked from one ruined room to the next. There was nothing in the whole of the historic house that she had not changed.

Nothing.

It felt like a metaphor for the way she had laid waste to Tadeo's own principles and self-regard.

Tadeo hated fucking metaphors.

Though as he walked through one atrium that bled into the next, with more floral theatrics at every turn, he knew that he could not lay that solely at her feet. The woman could be as wicked as she liked, but it was the wickedness in him that had met hers.

He was the one at fault. He accepted that.

Now he wished to be done with it. There was no doubt a sweet, unassuming, deeply boring heiress somewhere that he could marry and never think about again. She would do her job and leave him to his. They would have a pleasant, comfortable, smooth sort of life, marked by nothing but the milestones of their children and the peaceful prosperity of the kingdom.

He could almost taste it. All that was needed was the quietly amicable divorce he had planned, with tasteful statements to the press about going their separate ways with no acrimony and the best of wishes for the other's happiness, etcetera, and he could have peace at last.

At last.

On the other side of the ruined house, he stepped outside onto one of the back terraces and surveyed the gardens as they stretched out toward the horizon and the Pyrenees in the distance.

It did not take a degree in landscape architecture to realize that the gardens, too, had been changed.

In seven years, Esme had completely transformed the sophisticated, manicured gardens that previous queens who had lived here—excluding his mother, of course, who had never set foot on this property while the gleaming shores of the Côte d'Azur existed—had enjoyed. They had all taken pride in overseeing the tending of these gardens, always passing the torch along to keep them quiet, contemplative. A fitting place of respite for a queen. A place for meditation and relaxation.

There was nothing the least bit *relaxing* about the gardens greeting him now.

They were a deafening bugle of early spring exuberance.

There were daffodils and crocuses and cherry blossoms, and they were everywhere, bright and bold. Unseemly and overwhelming, Tadeo thought darkly, and he could not understand why he could not find a single, solitary soul to explain to him what was happening here.

He knew that Esme had not gone on a trip of any kind. Her schedule went through his office, for his review. The palace had only just begun taking on their outward-facing duties again as mourning for the late King had only this week come to an official end.

Esme should have been here. Doing whatever it was she did with her time.

Which was, he reflected now, wrecking heritage sites with the wanton application of tawdry colors slapped about with no thought whatsoever for the lines of the garden or its pathways or its internal logic, apparently.

He stood still in the not precisely warm air of the late February morning, generating more than enough heat on his own. The sun was already warm, hinting at the fairer months to come. The chill of winter almost felt like a memory when the sunlight moved over his face.

Tadeo needed her excised from this house, and the kingdom, and his life before another season passed. If he allowed himself the sort of dramatics he felt only when he was in Esme's vicinity, he would be tempted to think his own life depended on it.

"But I do not allow it," he growled out at himself. As a reminder he should not have needed, yet clearly did. Another reason this long, torturous chapter of his life needed to end.

He thought he heard a sound in the distance and he made himself walk toward it, scowling at the once-orderly flower beds everywhere, now showing no restraint or any evidence of planning. It was all too bright. Too out of control. As if someone had spun around in a circle like a child with bubbles, flinging seeds about.

The image he had then, of Esme doing exactly that, did not help his mood any.

Tadeo battled his way down an overgrown pathway where vines had been encouraged to do as they liked, making his way out toward the far end of the gardens, where a pergola sat between the garden proper and the start of the vineyards that some enterprising queen had insisted be grown here some while back. They did not produce a lot of wine, but every year, the queen's vintners produced a specialized run of limited-edition bottles of the queen's Pinot Noir. It had long been seen as something of a status symbol among certain sets in the kingdom's society.

Tadeo half expected to find the vines torn up and discarded in favor of an amusement park or something equally hideous, but they were still there. Waiting for the summer to ripen into grapes suitable for wine.

He heard voices again and strode toward them, feeling more and more like a storm cloud as he went.

Then he walked up through the vine-laden path to the pergola and found his wife at last.

She was sitting at the long table in the shade there with what appeared to be her own staff members. There was food and drink in platters, but there were also swathes of fabric, and Esme herself seemed to be wearing half of them.

It took him long, heart-pounding moments to realize that he was reacting to two things at once. One, he had no idea what they were doing, and no one seemed to look at his direction or even notice he was there, which was unusual. Two, and more concerning, it was impossible not to notice that Esme looked…well.

Very well.

Glowing, in fact.

And his body, his temple that he preferred to keep

completely under his control at all times like a bit of marble that he alone could sculpt, betrayed him yet again.

The way it had from the start where Esme was concerned.

Because every time he laid eyes on this woman, it was like he was burned alive. She was a poison in his blood, a curse upon his soul, and a great lamentation in the cock that he otherwise ruthlessly controlled. If *a great lamentation* was what to call it when he was nothing at all but hard and needy while the woman was doing nothing but sitting in a chair across a table from where he was standing, with very little of her visible aside from her face.

Damn her.

He waited. Esme didn't look up. She was talking animatedly to one of the women dressed in black beside her. They were both moving their fingers over the fabric that was swaddled all over as if they'd been draping it over Esme on purpose, but he couldn't hear what they were saying.

It was possible he had stood there a long while before a different woman altogether looked up, met Tadeo's gaze, and gasped.

"Your Majesty!" she cried.

He watched the ripple effect as it happened. First everyone froze. Then, as if lit by the same flame, all of the servants leaped to their feet—pushing back their chairs so there were loud scraping noises against the tile patio, then dropping into deep, deep curtsies.

His queen, Tadeo noticed—his *wife*, though hopefully not for much longer—did not rise, though it was protocol that she do so. Esme stayed where she was, draped in so many different shades of billowing fabric that he could barely see her body beneath it.

"Leave us," Tadeo told the staff, and did not watch them as they all fluttered off, like so many dark-feathered birds. He kept watching Esme. He studied her maddeningly perfect oval of a face with her dark flashing eyes and that lush, impossible mouth that he absolutely could not feel all over his body, because that was insupportable.

"Have you taken up sewing?" he asked her, not convinced he was entirely in control of his voice. He blamed her for that, too.

The proverbial straw on a camel's back.

"I'm redecorating a room," she replied.

In that same serene voice of hers. Brimming with that same abominable confidence that he found both atrocious and wildly compelling.

Tragically, she also remained the most beautiful woman he'd ever encountered.

This had been true when she was but a sophomore at Wellesley. It was even more true now. It was an outrage on every level, but she still looked like the model of the perfect woman, should he have been asked to draw such a creature.

Should *drawing* be one of his talents.

It was not that she was the most beautiful woman in the world, he supposed. But it was a cruel trick of fate that she managed to hit every single one of the buttons Tadeo had not entirely realized he had until he'd met her. She was elegant. She was graceful in everything, from her smallest gestures to the way she laughed—a sound that came from her belly and transformed her whole face. She had the sort of exquisite manners that were necessary for the circles they moved in, but Esme always made them seem as if they were innate.

As it was not something she was *doing*, but something that was simply a part of *who she was*.

She had been kind to his father, who had been less enticed by the *fairy-tale* argument and had been largely chilly in return. She was always kind to their subjects, no matter what sort of questions they tried to ask her while she was shaking hands and playing her part. It was his cross to bear that she also looked equally as stunning when she was in jeans and flats as she did in a bespoke gown made for ceremony and circumstance.

Today, she had her dark, glossy hair piled casually on the back of her head. It looked like she was wearing a simple T-shirt, which seemed to hug her curves more than usual. And yet she still simply emanated sophistication from every pore.

Only Tadeo knew that there were ways to touch this woman that lit her on fire. Only he knew what she looked like, her dark eyes glazed over with sex and longing, her mouth open while sounds of desire poured out, and how she writhed beneath him, taking more and more until he wasn't certain if either one of them would actually survive—

But that was not the point of this visit.

"My father has been dead for five months," he told her curtly.

"Five months and thirteen days," Esme replied. Oddly specific, to his mind, but she said it so calmly. Her lips curved. "I am aware, Tadeo."

If he could go back in time, he would not have given

her access to his family name. By the end, only his father still called him that in person. Most of his friends from school called him variations on his title. Or other nicknames of one sort or another.

The press, of course, used all of his names as they pleased.

He could have had her call him by his proper first name and he often thought that would be easier, because he wouldn't feel this tug of undeserved familiarity. Maybe the name alone would have done it. Maybe then he would never have become familiar with her at all.

But he couldn't go back to that first dinner in a quiet restaurant overlooking the Charles and fix what happened.

He could only do the necessary damage control now.

"I told you long ago that we would remain married only as long as necessary," he told her, no longer caring how dark he sounded. It needed to be done. It didn't matter *how* it was done. "I've come here to let you know that I intend to begin our divorce proceedings. Immediately."

Tadeo didn't know what he expected. For her to cheer, perhaps? Sometimes he convinced himself that she was no more interested in continuing this marriage of theirs than he was. Perhaps he thought she might cry? After all, he hadn't been so far gone that he'd forgotten the things she'd whispered in the night after his father's death.

Sometimes he thought those words haunted him.

But of all the possible responses he'd imagined, it wasn't the way she smiled at him.

Her lips curved gently. Even kindly, he thought.

And then she rose.

The fabric cascaded off her and slid in heaps of shimmering color to either side of her, landing on the tiles at her feet.

But Tadeo forgot all about that. He couldn't take his eyes off her.

Because the Esme he had last seen five months ago had been lean and lithe and in some way resembled the ballet dancer she had once told him she would have liked to have become, in a different life.

She stood, the fabric fell, and she placed her hand on the shelf of the belly—*her belly*—that had swelled up to enormous size. A great deal as if she had a ball beneath her shirt, when, of course, she did not.

It was impossible. It was inconceivable.

It was a disaster of epic proportions and she was *smiling—*

"About that divorce," Esme said, as if they were discussing the weather. Or what to have the staff prepare for a snack. As if she was not very obviously *pregnant*. "I wonder if you might want to rethink."

CHAPTER TWO

Esme could admit that she found the look on Tadeo's face deeply satisfying, whatever that might have said about her as a person. She accepted that it likely said nothing good.

And yet there it was, just the same. Pure satisfaction, sweeping through her like a small, personal tsunami.

She had anticipated that this moment would please her when it came—and she'd known it would come eventually—but she had to admit that this far exceeded her expectations. Esme would not go so far as to say it made up for the past five months of self-recrimination, worry, and intense doubt, but it certainly felt like a gesture in that direction.

After all, she'd been expecting him for a long while now.

At first, she'd thought that he might come sooner. Right after that night in the palace, when the passion that he'd been denying for seven years had finally boiled over in that mess of grief and comfort…and what she thought was simply humanity at its most basic. What people did when they were still alive and someone they'd loved was dead.

But he didn't, because he was made of ice when he wanted to be. So frigid it was a wonder flowers could even grow in this kingdom.

Then she'd been certain that he would make it happen at different times over the past few months. After he got back on his feet in the wake of the funeral. After he soothed the nation with his careful speeches from the iconic Bellazan throne room, promising his rule would be what they'd come to expect from his father—smooth and peaceful. After he figured out every last in and out of his new position, which shouldn't have been *too* overwhelming or taxing for him, all things considered. Since he had been training for it since the day he was born.

It had taken her a long while to accept that he was really going to wait as long as possible to face what had happened that night. To come to the bitter conclusion that he had no intention of addressing it, only of divorcing her.

In the meantime, of course, she'd had other things to think about. More pressing things, as said things were growing inside her.

"How is this possible?" asked the man himself now, after a satisfyingly long while looking *stunned*. The way a cartoon character looked when struck with a shovel, she rather thought. She'd never seen Tadeo look like that before. She would have said it was impossible.

But then, their entire history was studded with impossibilities, one after the next—so what was another one tossed on top?

Esme was distressed to find that he was still as offensively gorgeous as ever. He had not lost all of his hair. He had not shrunk down from his more than six feet. He had not lost that rangy, athletic physique of his that made it seem as if he spent significant hours of his life roaming about playing sports of one kind or another when she knew full well he did not. He was the king now and had previously been a very visible and involved crown prince. He could not be racing about playing football—soccer, when he'd been in the States—the way he had in his youth.

Sadly for her, he still possessed that chiseled male beauty and the most beautiful face she had ever seen on a man in her life. He had those remarkably blue eyes. That thick brown hair that wanted desperately to curl when he wasn't being so stern and austere. That impossibly perfect jaw with a *dimple*, no less, on the rare occasions he smiled.

That dimple had been her undoing.

More than once.

There was no sign of it today. Tadeo was wearing one of his casual outfits, such as it was. Esme was in a soft pair of maternity jeans to hold her precious belly, but His Majesty preferred not to wear jeans at all. He found them *déclassé*.

He had told her that shortly after their wedding as if she couldn't remember him wearing them back in Boston. All the time.

Here in Bellaza he preferred dark trousers. They were actually cargo pants today, and clung lovingly to his unduly powerful thighs. He was wearing what she supposed was technically a sweatshirt, but was of course of such fine construction and made from such intensely exquisite fabric that it fell over his exquisite chest like cashmere.

Esme's whole life would be completely different right now if this man had been even slightly unattractive.

She thought about this all the time.

If she had simply found him pleasant, if the conversation had been stilted that first night. If he hadn't reached over, that wondering sort of smile on his beautiful face with that *dimple* in evidence and that intensity in his blue gaze, then picked up her hand—

They would be different people. She would probably still be here, in this house of exile on the palace grounds, but she imagined she'd be resigned to it. And happier for it. Or they would have committed to one of those dreadfully common marriages of cold convenience, with separate rooms and scheduled copulation for the making of heirs, with a happy retreat into polite if distant companionship thereafter. Not unlike the marriage they'd had, really—except notably devoid of all the seething tension that had always underscored even their most seemingly polite interactions.

Tadeo scowled at her. "Do you intend to answer my question, Esme?"

She ordered herself to stop thinking about *copulation*. And his ruinous dimple. "I beg your pardon. I thought that was facetious at best." She studied him. "How do you think it happened, Tadeo?"

"But…" She had never seen this man flustered. Furious, yes. Cracking at the seams, certainly. Wild with passion, temper, emotion. All the things she had learned since that he deplored. She had seen all of that. But she'd never seen him simply…flustered. Yet today she thought that was exactly what he was. "But back in Boston…"

She thought she could hear his teeth grinding together. No doubt because he was physically allergic to admitting that they had, in fact, been in Boston. Together. Intimately.

"Are you…referencing our secret, scandalous past?" she asked in a very sweet tone that was not all that sweet. "Heaven forfend! Next thing you know, you'll be acknowledging that it actually happened, and then where would we be?"

"You didn't get pregnant then," he gritted out, a flash of something in his gaze that made her think that he was remembering that breathless year, the sheets they'd torn up, the pleasure they'd found—

But Boston was not the issue here. Not today.

"Of course I didn't get pregnant then." She folded her hands over her belly bump and allowed herself to enjoy the little things right here and now. Like this moment that felt a bit like schadenfreude. "Perhaps one of the numerous things you've conveniently forgotten about that time is how much we both wanted—"

"I do not want to discuss the details of those days," he bit out. Confirming that he was indeed remembering the same things she was, she rather thought. "They are like a fever dream I do not wish to revisit now that the worst of the illness is past."

"So you have mentioned," she said, soothingly, as if he was a fractious child. It had the effect she expected it would. He glowered.

But for years, that had been the closest she could get to the passion she remembered. The passion that sometimes woke her in the night to fume in her empty bed.

Or, some years, cry.

She would act the part required of her, poke at him a

little, and call it a result when he responded in some way. In any way. And so had seven years gone by, somehow.

Yes, she was enjoying this today. It felt like payback. After all, he was *so* shocked. As if he hadn't been a full and enthusiastic participant in the act that led to this. "Let me set the scene for you. Two people meet and their attraction is overwhelming, outrageous. Life-altering, some might say."

"Esme."

"I know *you* wouldn't say that. Now." He scowled and she kept going. "Yet both of them knew that they had degrees to finish, kingdoms not to disappoint, and so on. They spent their first two weeks together in an agony of extended foreplay—"

"*Esme*. Why must you always do this? I do not wish to wallow in these memories you seem to want to trot out at the slightest provocation—"

"I was on the pill, Tadeo," she told him coolly. "I got on the pill the morning after our first meeting, and it worked. After our wedding, when you informed me that I would be imprisoned in this marriage until the day your father died and then summarily released, I saw no particular reason to continue playing games with my hormones. I went off the pill then. And here we are."

"You knew that you were not using birth control," he said, sounding as if he was being extremely careful with his words, likely because he thought they might detonate. Or he would. "You knew, and yet—"

"Be very careful, Tadeo," Esme advised him then. "You are straying perilously close to blaming me for a night in which both of us were drinking the very same alcohol from the very same bottle, and then made the very same choice. Perhaps you should question yourself."

"I've questioned myself every night since."

"Marvelous." She clasped her hands together. "Then you have already taken yourself to task for not handling the birth control options yourself. Either way, here we are. I am five months and thirteen days pregnant. If you would like to go ahead and divorce me, I won't stop you. That might even be best."

Her clasped hands folded nicely, so she did that and then propped them up on her belly again. Esme made herself smile, as beatifically as possible. Then when all he did was glower in her direction, she kept going. "I've had a lot of time to think about it, and I do think it might be best. I'm happy to divorce. You can continue doing… whatever self-flagellation exercises it is that you prefer. I can have a life. And our child can have the attention of both of its parents without having to worry about living in the ice fjords of the palace here." She considered. "Or at least not full-time."

"You might have had a lot of time to think about this, but I have had not." *Flustered*, she thought again, as he raked his hands through his hair. It made her wonder if he would ever grow it out again the way he had when he was a graduate student in a foreign land. And the other occupant of her bed.

After their affair had ended, he'd cut it all off.

She'd seen it in a tabloid and had cried for days.

"You can have all the time you need," she told him serenely now, as if bestowing upon him a great gift. "That said, there is a ticking clock." She patted her belly. "Like it or not."

Tadeo glared at her for what felt like a very long time. His gaze swept over her, from the top of her head to as much of her as he could see from his side of the table.

Esme could have told him that she'd been sitting out here playing with fabrics, imagining the nursery in this house. She had decided with the help of the staff members here, who had all become her friends, that it would be best to decorate it. To celebrate the baby and her impending motherhood while they all waited for that other shoe to fall.

They had all known that it would. Esme had told them from the start that if they felt it necessary to confess her condition to the King, she would understand. At the end of the day, they worked for him. Everyone in the kingdom did.

Especially her.

But not one of her staff had taken her up on that. Over the years, they'd become close. With the occasional addition of her friends from college, who would sometimes fly in and brighten things up for a while, the staff here were Esme's daily support.

Her parents were only a mountain range away, and supported her in all things, but she never wanted them to think that they'd made a mistake in setting up this marriage. She never wanted to worry them. She still didn't. In fact, she worked hard to convince them that everything in her marriage was fine. Perfectly *fine*—and she assumed her perceptive mother chose to believe her. Because her mother loved her.

We can see about confessions when His Majesty chooses to visit, the housekeeper had said tartly one morning, waiting for Esme outside the bathroom suite in her rooms. The older woman had held out the ginger drink they'd made for her on those early pregnancy mornings when her stomach wanted to separate itself from her body. As violently as possible. *But he would have to come here in order to do that, would he not?*

Esme could tell Tadeo all that. She could tell him what the past seven years had been like, sequestered in this manor house and trotted out only to smile and wave and play her part, all while pretending she felt nothing for him outside of the roles they played. But why start there? That was simply how long they'd been married.

She could go back even further. To having to drag herself through her final year of college utterly heartbroken, a ghost of her former self, because he had dropped her so cruelly. Her friends had rallied. They had done their best, but they didn't understand—and how could she explain?—that the situations with college boys they loved and would forget that they were comparing to her affair with Tadeo were different. Not as intense. Not as all-consuming. Not as *real*.

There was no way to share those things, even though she knew it was true. It would only make her sound delusional.

Esme had become so embarrassed by the fact that she couldn't seem to find her smile again that she'd forced it. She'd figured out how she could always put on a face appropriate to the moment, no matter what she was feeling inside. She'd learned how to play whatever role was needed and expected, with no one the wiser.

This new ability got her through graduation, then off to London for a charity internship that had been plotted out long ago. Princess Esme of Clarebonne had made a few tasteful charity-based headlines that year and at the end of it, she had been certain that she would be left to explain to her parents, her own kingdom—and his— that there would be no fairy-tale betrothal after all. That just because their families had agreed that there would be one, one day, and had even hinted in public at their being betrothed from her birth, it would never happen. She'd been preparing her statement since college.

Esme had been nothing short of flabbergasted when she'd received formal notice from his kingdom that the royal courtship would begin.

Maybe, finally, she could tell him what it had been like to have to succumb to an extremely public relationship, every moment scripted for the cameras, with the ex who had ripped her heart out of her body and stomped it into dust. Like it was nothing.

But she doubted he wanted to hear any of that.

Now, she watched him turn away from her, looking back over the gardens that she had made her own. They were happy now. Bright explosions of color, basking in their own beauty. She treated the manor house itself the same way. Every time he made her sad, she found something else to brighten. Room by room, wall by wall, she put bright colors in place of the parts of her heart that he'd bruised.

She couldn't say that she regretted it.

"This isn't what I had planned either, you know," she said, addressing his back. His outrageously well-muscled back that, if she let herself think about it too much, she could actually *feel* beneath her fingertips. As if she was wrapped around him, holding him close, her fingers digging into his shoulder blades as he surged deep inside her—

The trouble with being pregnant, she had discovered, was that—contrary to what she'd always believed, given the way people talked about the state—she did not feel at all like that beaming, sexless, goddess mother figure she'd expected would take her over.

All she thought about was sex. Not just any kind of sex. Specifically, sex with Tadeo.

It was a torment.

His being here today didn't exactly help.

He didn't respond to her, so she kept going. "I was looking forward to our divorce. I was going to move back to the States. Do some good work with my time. Help others, perhaps launch a lifestyle cooking show, whatever came to mind. I thought perhaps I would find a chic home in Manhattan like Jackie Onassis and swan about with oversize sunglasses for the rest of my life, refusing interviews. Either way, the world was mine." She blew out a breath. "But somehow I think that's no longer the option that it was."

Her friends had been more and more adamant on every visit over the years. She needed to get the hell out of Bellaza. She had to get as far away as it was possible to get from King Tadeo.

That man has been a shadow over your entire life and has blocked out your sun since you were twenty, her best friend, Hilary, had said matter-of-factly. *It's been too long, Esme. It's time for something new.*

Esme had agreed. And instead, she was pregnant. Not just pregnant the way anyone might be, *she* was pregnant with the baby who would be heir to the kingdom of Bellaza and there was precious little possibility that anyone in the palace or this valley would look kindly on that heir being raised on a separate continent. So that was that.

A full eclipse, I'm afraid, she'd told Hilary.

Tadeo turned back to her and though there was a glittering in his gaze, his face remained unreadable. When there had been a time, long ago now, that she'd been able to read him so easily.

"I will concede we are both to blame for this," he said, sounding darkly formal and so stuffy it made her want to scream. But that would be playing into his narrative about her—so emotional, so immature, so over-the-top, and so on—so she smiled instead. "It is both of our faults."

"I understand that you are getting used to this," she said in the same soothing tone she'd been using, that she hoped he found condescending. "You've had a shock and you'll need some time with it. That's acceptable. But I'm not going to stand around and talk about the child *we made*, who will be coming into this world in not so many months, as something we should be ashamed of. Or call it a fault or a mistake. I just want that very clear."

"I wasn't the one who kept it a secret," he replied with that cold efficiency that had always left her breathless. It was like a knife. "Have you seen a physician?"

"No, I thought that it would be great fun to simply risk everything and see what happened," Esme shot back at him. When his eyes widened slightly, she sighed. "Of course I've seen a physician. The same physician I always see."

"You mean the palace physician." When she nodded,

Tadeo looked astonished. "And no report was made to me?"

"I imagine the palace physician was under the impression you already knew," Esme said coolly. "Since you are, in fact, my husband."

"You knew that I did not."

"I saw no reason to tell you." Esme shrugged. "You made your position very clear. You told me to leave the palace and not to return unless and until I was summoned. That you would tell my people when that was and that you did not want to lay eyes on me until that occurred. I listened."

She had not only listened. She had finally accepted, deep in her poor battered heart, that there would never be the kind of future she wanted with this man.

It had hurt almost as much as losing him the first time, but she'd gotten there. She knew he'd meant it when he'd said he would divorce her. He'd meant it when he'd said it before their wedding and he'd meant it even more when he'd reiterated it the morning after his father's funeral. Esme had mourned that spark of hope she'd carried inside all this while, truly she had. But she had finally started to think about what life might be like *without* this particular shadow blotting out the sun.

And then she'd discovered she was pregnant.

Esme found that empathy for him in this moment felt scarce on the ground.

His gaze went cold. His jaw clenched. "You know perfectly well that I didn't mean you should hide the fact that you were *pregnant*."

Esme lifted her chin. "I don't know that. I only know what you said, Tadeo. Isn't that something that you were at great pains to make me understand years ago? You only wished to discuss what you *said*. Not how your actions might have been received and certainly not how the way you said those things might have made someone else *feel*."

"I do not wish to discuss Boston," he said then, in that low, furious voice of his that reminded her—violently—of that hideous day when he'd told her he was done with her. And had meant it then, too.

It still made her whole body flush. It still *hurt*, and she hated herself for that, but he didn't deserve to see that any longer. So she smiled instead.

Because she was so damned good at smiling.

"Here in the house of exile," she said, with an airiness that actually hurt, "I talk about whatever I wish. If you would like to direct the conversation, decide what words are used, and determine what eras are worthy of discussion, you can go back to the palace and order everyone about to your heart's content. Your Majesty."

Something flared on his face at that and Esme caught her breath, because for just a moment she could see the Tadeo that she knew. The Tadeo she missed. The hint of him, right there—

But he pulled it back. He hid it away. And then he stepped back as if she'd thrown herself over the table and tried to touch him.

As if she'd be so foolish after all these years.

She really had learned. At last.

"I am not going to process this information in real time with you," he told her, with scathing formality. "Certainly not while you clearly wish to make my doing so as painful as possible. You'll hear from my people soon."

Then he turned sharply, as if he was back in the military service he'd done after graduate school, and marched away.

Esme watched him go. She took in that straight line of his back and the powerful way he moved until he disappeared into a riot of bright yellow daffodils, happy purple crocuses, and reckless sprays of forsythia.

She watched him until he was gone and then, when she was alone again, all of her masks and coping mechanisms tumbled at her feet like so much more slippery fabric for the nursery of a child who deserved better than all this acrimony.

As she sat down in her chair, cradled her head in her arms, and, despite her best intentions to banish the shadows from her life, sobbed.

CHAPTER THREE

THE SUMMONS FROM the palace came the next morning, bright and early.

The housekeeper brought it in with Esme's breakfast, which was happily no longer a few dry crackers and a ginger drink. Her appetite had come roaring back with a vengeance once she made it into the second trimester, and having sorely missed it, she liked to indulge it. Her cook liked to tempt her with various breakfast dishes and today it was some kind of frittata, fluffy and cheesy, and she tucked in with pleasure.

But the heavy envelope from the palace was there the whole time, a baleful presence in her otherwise happy, lovely room. She stared at it, sitting there on its own silver platter, and ignored it while she ate.

It was still a habit to wait to see if her stomach would behave, even though she hadn't had a morning sickness episode in weeks. When she'd first experienced it, she'd thought she had some sort of flu or cold that wouldn't go away. Not unusual during the cold months of the year, and she'd assumed that she was simply run-down. Or that it was her body's reaction to seven years of royal appointments and public engagements, forever playing the part of the perfect queen for an adoring public and having to act like the frozen iceberg beside her when in private with him.

Esme had been fond of the excruciatingly formal and distinctly chilly King Hugo, despite his best attempts to cut her down to size. She would not say that she'd managed to charm the man, but she thought he'd come to accept her—and clearly approved of the separate lives she and Tadeo led on the palace grounds, which only palace denizens knew. She had even come to see that the old man had a certain charm that she'd seen in his son, too, if long ago. She had genuinely mourned his death, but it had still taken her much too long to realize what she was feeling was not simply illness or grief.

Then there had been coming to terms with what it *meant* that she was pregnant. That had taken longer.

Especially because she had finally been at peace with leaving this place, and Tadeo, and starting over.

When her stomach indicated that it intended to stay in place again today, Esme rose from her bed. Still not touching that envelope, she puttered around through her usual morning routine, but when it came time to choose something to wear, she stopped. Blew out a breath. Then accepted the inevitable and picked up the small, square envelope that felt as if it was lined with metal and was actually sealed with wax.

Because here in Bellaza there was a right way and a wrong way to do things, and the right way very often involved archaic rituals.

She cracked open the seal and pulled out the card. And then accepted that she was disappointed when she saw that the message inside was typed. More importantly, it was not in Tadeo's bold, dark hand.

The Queen's presence is requested at the palace, it said. Baldly.

No time. No date. Just a request that was not a request at all. It was an order.

Esme did not pretend that she didn't understand that.

She walked into her dressing room, a large, expansive room with alcove offshoots that featured accessories of all descriptions. Many of the clothes no longer fit. She slid her hand over her belly and found herself feeling sentimental about the press of it into her palm.

Esme had rather given up on the idea of children. Or maybe it was more accurate to say that it was one of the many things she'd put into a deep freeze, because it was that or spend more time sobbing about futures that could never be hers.

She had decided on her chilly—so beautiful, but so personally *cold*—wedding day that she had a choice to make. It was clear to her that nothing would change between her and this brand-new husband of hers who had already smashed her heart into smithereens more times than she could count. It was true that she'd held out hope that he might have had ulterior motives for going through with all this, but that day, she'd known better.

His kingdom had been promised Princess Esme of Clarebonne and Tadeo, by God, would give her to them. Without regard for her feelings or his own, assuming he had any left in there somewhere. For on their wedding day, he had informed her that he planned to shunt her off to a separate house so it would not be necessary for them to lay eyes on each other for any reason but work.

The choice she'd had to make was all too obvious. She could let him hurt her over and over again by simple dint of his insensitivity and coldness and *absolute refusal* to admit what she knew to be true about the things that had happened between them in Boston. Esme had been all too able to envision that future. Forever smashing her head against the brick wall of him. Over and over again, hurting only herself, and to what end?

The other option was the one she'd chosen. She prided herself on playing the perfect princess, now queen. She was kind, warm, unfailingly polite and courteous at all times. The kingdom loved her. Her own kingdom was deeply proud of her. The papers fell all over themselves to praise her quiet elegance and her endless charity. Everyone was in awe of her ability to remember the name of every person she'd ever met, make every person she interacted with feel special, and to always support her husband as well as King Hugo.

She did these things not only because she was good at them, though she was, but because she rather thought that Tadeo expected her to descend into a tantrum and never emerge from it again.

Esme kept her emotions at the manor house. That was the place where she allowed herself any outlets that she liked for the things she couldn't let herself feel anywhere else. Whether it was tantrums on the floor, screaming into her pillows, or experimenting with paint. Or all of the above, on particularly bad days.

It wasn't the life she'd imagined they'd have, all those years ago in Boston when it had seemed miraculous that they were so well-suited when they'd been promised to each other sight unseen, but it worked.

Now all of the rules she'd lived by for seven years seemed out the window. They'd gone straight up in smoke the night of the funeral, when she'd finally touched him again the way she had only when they'd been across an ocean and everything had been different—

She'd had time to regret that. And to…not regret it at all, to an epic degree.

But the trouble was, she knew Tadeo. She knew him better than she wanted to, most of the time. His response to this would not be to finally open up, meet her halfway, and pledge himself to working on making himself a better man, husband, and soon-to-be father. Open, giving, emotionally available.

Esme laughed out loud in her dressing room. "Whatever he has planned is far more likely to involve the palace's medieval dungeons," she said to herself.

Then laughed again, because how would *dungeons* play in the press Tadeo cared so much about? She couldn't wait to find out. How would his team handle *that* messaging?

She turned around in a circle, her eyes narrow as she looked at her image in the mirror, deciding how best to approach a meeting that she assumed would be more of a chess match. She settled on a very simple and casual dress in royal blue that hugged all of her curves—so that there could be no mistake about the state of her body. Then, to forestall any commentary that she might have dressed down in a jersey midi dress in defiance of his beloved protocol, she accessorized with a full face of makeup and chunky jewelry.

The better to send conflicting messages. The Queen was off-duty today, yes—but she was still the Queen.

Esme considered walking to the palace but rejected it, as she didn't wish to appear before Tadeo flushed from exertion. That it would irritate him made it tempting, but she was afraid she would end up feeling too flustered. That wouldn't do. She called to have a car brought around and drove herself over, trying her best to settle her nerves and her mind. Both were racing, because whatever else might be happening, she was still excited to see him.

It had always been this way. Since the moment she'd met him—and if she was honest, before that, too. She had never minded that she was promised to someone. She had always thought it was romantic, though she doubted she would have felt that way if the man she'd been promised to had been something other than outrageously handsome, with those impossible blue eyes, a jawline to write poetry about, and that body of his that he kept in such peak physical condition—

But that was not a good way to keep herself from coming over all *flushed*.

At the palace, the guards directed her to drive back around to one of the family entrances, which was what they called the secret passageways with covered entries that allowed members of the royal family and any guests or companions they wished to keep secret to come and go as they liked. No photographic evidence. No crowds or watchful eyes.

She pulled up in her car and the King's personal secretary was there to greet her, stiffly. Always stiffly. The proper older man could fade into the wallpaper if he chose, disappearing in plain sight. He had been here forever. He knew everything about everyone, and more.

Esme was even happier that she was wearing a dress that made her condition so clear.

If the old man noticed Esme's pregnancy, she would never know from his demeanor—but she knew that he did. He noticed everything. It was his job.

"How interesting that I need a personal escort today," Esme said merrily as she left the car for the staff to move where they liked. "Does the King think that I am likely to foment rebellion on my way to see him?"

"If Your Majesty would watch your step," replied the studiously unbothered Arturo, as he held the door for her.

Esme trailed after him once inside, trying not to let herself become too emotional. It was difficult, but she couldn't blame her hormones entirely. She had been emotional the first time she'd walked into this palace too. It had been before their wedding and she'd still had that reckless core of hope deep inside her—

But that was long gone. She tried to shake the memory off as she followed docilely enough behind Arturo as he led her deep into the palace.

Having grown up in the palace next door—give or take a few mountain ranges—Esme had always thought that the Bellazan palace felt like a fairy tale. It was all about its spires and flourishes, with dramatic details in every direction. Her father's palace was far more utilitarian, more of a civic expression of royalty than an ideal.

She would never admit this to her own people, but she preferred the Bellazan palace to the Clarebonne one. This one was prettier. Airier. It made her want to sing songs and spin about, not that she ever had. It would be frowned upon.

Luckily, she thought as they walked, its inhabitants made up for their lovely fairy-tale palace by being as dour as humanly possible.

Arturo took her on a route that, she couldn't help but notice, avoided all the main thoroughfares of the palace where anyone might see her. Then delivered her into a salon in the family wing where only one person could possibly see her and left her there, with a deep and proper bow as he exited.

She wandered over to the window and gazed out of it, looking at the hills in the distance. The small principality of Andorra was to the south. Her own Clarebonne to the east, Spain to the west, France to the north.

It struck her then that her own world had become quite small these last five months.

"I was nesting," she said under her breath, defending herself. "And sleeping."

And mourning kings and lives lost in more than one way.

Then again, she thought as the door opened behind her and her whole body reacted—indicating at once that Tadeo had entered the room—it was possible that she had been preparing for battle.

She turned to look at him.

Today he'd chosen the typical dark, bespoke suit. His usual fare. And also his armor, she thought. She stood where she was, smiling gently as he let his gaze track all over her—lingering on her belly, of course.

And had the satisfaction of watching his jaw clench.

"I apologize for my emotional outbursts yesterday," he said without any preamble, and he didn't even sound stiff. Though he also didn't sound all that sorrowful. "It won't happen again."

"I should think not," she replied calmly. "That would mean you might actually have to feel things, and we can't have that."

That blue gaze of his went frigid, but he did not reply. Instead, he moved to take one of the seats, gesturing for her to do the same.

Esme thought about resisting, but decided against it for strategic reasons when there were far bigger things to worry about. She went and sat so she was facing him across an exquisite little table made of glass with dramatic leg flourishes. So cozy. So intimate.

Such bullshit.

She imagined it had taken most of his team to decide on this room. They would have debated it. Would the austerity of his office be the wrong touch? Was the royal glory of the more formal rooms too aspirational? She hoped that he was up half the night concerned with the messaging of this.

Tadeo was always preoccupied with his *messaging*.

"I will confess to you that I did not make any provision for something so unforeseen to occur in this marriage," he continued in the same relatively friendly voice, despite the chill in his gaze.

Esme gazed back at him. "Points for sounding so human, Tadeo. How long did you practice that? You sound sincere and slightly self-deprecating. The faint smile is a nice touch as well."

Said faint smile disappeared immediately. "I'm trying to have a conversation with you."

"No," she replied steadily. "You are not. You are trying to manage me. They are not the same thing."

"I'm not going to have a semantic battle with you, Esme," Tadeo replied, sounding significantly more like himself. Which was to say, a lofty robot.

"I don't think that pointing out the reality of a thing is a battle," Esme said, sitting back in her chair. "Unless, of course, one of the people in this room is overly committed to protecting a reality that does not exist." She patted her belly. "That couldn't be me. Reality is growing inside of me, by the day, whether I like it or not."

"It has always been my intention to divorce you, as you know," he replied, something like steel around his eyes.

"The topic has come up a time or two, yes," Esme agreed, warmly enough that she hoped it covered that spike of *hurt* she wished she didn't feel any longer. Yet did. "But then, you wouldn't be you if you weren't planning your escape before you walked into a room. I do believe that some people refer to that as a trauma response, Tadeo. Have you ever considered—"

"When I want your psychoanalysis, Esme, I will ask for it. You may note that I never have."

She inclined her head. "Please," she said, smiling wider. "Don't let me keep you from opining on the state of our marriage. I do love these chats. They are like quarterly performance reviews. Or better yet, like small, sweet love notes tucked into my life at these delightfully random intervals. I can't tell you how I look forward to them."

Tadeo studied her for a long moment, his face impressively impassive. In the beginning, she'd been able to get a frown out of him. These days she had to content herself with that flexed muscle in his jaw.

This was part of why her performance as the Princess, now Queen, of Bellaza required such a commitment to perfection. The more beautifully she did her part, the more outrageously she could behave in private.

A girl had to have her fun somewhere.

"This ruins my plans," he told her. After some while.

Esme felt an actual flare of temper at that, but she had years of practice batting such things down. "I beg your pardon. Do you mean to say that your child, the heir to your throne, has destroyed the plans you made in your head? That's a strange way indeed to say congratulations, Tadeo. Even for you."

"I like to tell myself that there is a perfect heiress out there." He leaned forward as he said this, his blue gaze heavy on hers, so Esme could make no mistake. He *wanted* her to hear him on this. To well and truly *hear him*. "When I think of her, her features themselves are blurry. Because it doesn't matter. What matters is how she will *act*. She will be quiet. Accepting. Meek in all things. She will not be emotional, or arch, or forever making attempts to be witty."

Esme allowed herself to frown slightly, as if picturing this saint among women. "She sounds deeply boring." She clucked her tongue. "The poor thing. Send her to me and I'll teach her how to live a little. It's necessary when married to an animated plank of wood to make one's own fun, you see."

Tadeo did not react. He continued to list off this made-up heiress's manufactured virtues. "She will be soft-spoken in both public and private. She will never make demands. She will be practical enough and clever enough to understand her place."

"She sounds like *quite* the paragon." If Esme felt these words of his—this description of the perfect wife he insisted on painting—like a small, wickedly sharp dagger to the heart, she kept it to herself. "I wish you every happiness, Tadeo, assuming that is one of the three emotions you allow yourself to feel annually. Does that mean we're going ahead with the divorce?"

"You know perfectly well that we cannot," he retorted. "And so I must give up on this perfect paragon of a queen and make do with you instead."

Esme wanted to scream so she smiled at him instead. "A fate worse than death."

"I struggle with how best to arrange this unforeseen situation to its best advantage," he said after a moment, no longer *spearing her* with that look of his.

"You keep calling it that." Esme shook her head. "I do hope you get that out of your system. I don't think that I will find it amusing if you call our child an *unforeseen circumstance* to its face."

"I understand that this is all a grand joke to you," Tadeo said, and he leaned forward then. And more surprising, he looked…*undone*, somehow. Everything inside Esme thrilled at that, though she knew better than to show it. "But it is not a joke to me."

"If you had to suffer through morning sickness for three solid months, with bits of it thereafter as a little treat when you least expect it, I doubt you would think it was all that funny yourself, Tadeo," she murmured in reply.

He ignored that. "You persist in poking at me whenever you can. You think it's amusing. I do not. I have certain obligations—"

"I am aware of your obligations." Esme rolled her eyes. "This entire speech worked better when I was barely twenty-one, and in case you're laboring under a misconception, I didn't really like it all that much then."

"Things will be different now," he told her, that ruthlessness she sometimes thought only she'd ever seen in him making his voice low and dark. "I will not tolerate these displays of yours that you trot out, presumably for your own entertainment."

Her heart skipped a few beats, then sped up, the way it had when he'd shown her this side of himself the first time. So many years ago, she'd thought she was having a heart attack. She'd wondered if losing him might actually kill her.

Now she knew there were much worse things than dying of a broken heart, and one of them was living with it. Another was marrying the man who'd broken it. Repeatedly.

Survival meant she'd learned how to ignore her heart when it beat like this, so she could soothe it when she was alone.

"And what exactly will you do?" Esme waved a languid hand, the very picture of someone completely unbothered by this. By him. "Will you march your pregnant wife, your queen and the mother of your heir, down into the dank recesses of your dungeon? However will that play in the press, Tadeo? Do you think it's possible that an out-of-control, raging king who's decided a pregnant woman is the enemy might finally be more scandalous than a very boring story about a woman who wanted extramarital—"

"Do not bring up my mother," he growled.

But Esme had long since decided that the much-maligned Queen Marisol was not an off-limits topic. She had decided that Tadeo could not use his mother as an excuse for everything he did and then refuse to hear her mentioned in return. Not that she had found many opportunities to put this decision into practice.

There was no time like the present.

She leaned forward. "Do you think it will work?"

His eyes glittered. It was obvious that he didn't want to answer the question.

"Will what work?" he asked, as if it made his jaw hurt to get the words out. She hoped it did.

"Do you think that your perfect, anodyne heiress will wash away your mother's grievous sins at last? Or do you just not wish to be reminded of them when you sit in a private room with another woman who dares speak her own mind?"

She didn't expect him to move. Maybe he didn't expect to move himself.

But one moment she was sitting in the seat opposite him, and the next, he was there. He braced himself above her, caging her in place with one arm on either side of her as his hands gripped the arms of the chair.

"How many warnings do you think I am going to give you?" he demanded, his face—his outrageously perfect face—far too close to hers.

"You don't want to feel anything," Esme said, tipping her head back so she could truly look him in the eye. "You take it as a personal failing when you have a stray emotion. I can't help you with that. I don't *want* to help you with that. But I do think, Tadeo, that you might want to consider the fact that fatherhood is not an unemotional state. Your child is not likely to respect your boundaries."

"Not with you to teach him he shouldn't," Tadeo gritted out.

"Do you think the babies you might have with your perfect windup doll of a queen would be any better?" Esme asked and she laughed a little, right there in his face. It had gotten easier over the years—or so she told herself—to ignore how beautiful this man was. But it was not easy now, with his face so close to hers. Not when she could remember kissing him months instead of *years* ago. Putting her hands on his jaw, pressing her lips to his, indulging herself in him the way she hadn't in so very, very long…

"I think everything would be better with the woman who was less…" He shook his head, eyes glittering. "With a woman who was not you, Esme."

"But the woman you described would never suit you," she said, and she laughed again. He didn't need to know that it felt like glass broken into pieces in her mouth. "I don't know why you're pretending otherwise."

"I think any man dreams of peace, king or not." She could smell the faint hint of that scent he always wore. The scent she had always found maddening, overwhelming, addictive. It was something that reminded her of wood smoke with a brighter note beneath. Pine, perhaps. Rosemary. "You wouldn't understand."

"But I do," Esme said. "It's never going to happen." She lifted a brow, and kept her gaze trained on his. "You like fucking too much for your little saint, my love."

His eyes flared. And she'd used all of those words deliberately. *Fucking*, to get his attention. *My love*, to remind of the thing he wanted to remember least.

She didn't see any reason why he should get to forget the thing she couldn't help but remember, like it or not. Especially when he was the one who took that love they'd shared and shattered it.

How could he have told her he loved her—again and again—and then act as if she'd made that up in her head? She would never know. She only knew that he'd done it.

He'd done it. Brutally. And she had been living with it ever since.

Esme could see the way he sucked in a breath and she leaned forward, her chin high and defiant. "You like to deny yourself like a monk or indulge yourself in me, but I doubt you've admitted the truth to yourself yet. That no matter what, it's not going away. It's still me. It's always going to be me."

She could see the way his hands clenched hard on the chair's arms, and kept going. "You hold yourself back, you capitulate, it's all the same. What you have never known, nor ever will, I fear, is peace. Exchanging me for a more biddable model won't help you. Because I will still exist." She angled herself toward him, letting the intensity between them lead. "So unless you're going to kill me? I'm afraid, Your Royal Majesty, that you're stuck."

"Damn you," he growled at her, but then he made it worse.

Or better, depending, Esme thought in a rush.

Because he crashed his mouth to hers.

CHAPTER FOUR

Esme was a fire in his blood, all bright colors and wild songs in his head.

She tasted the way she always had—too good to believe. An impossible, immediate addiction that he had always felt as keenly as if she was an injection straight into his veins.

Sometimes he thought he hated her for showing him that it was even possible to feel like this.

And he knew he hated her more because she wasn't afraid to turn him inside out and lay out all his weaknesses before him. So he could not continue to tell himself stories that cast him as the hero.

Once upon a time, he knew that he'd found that sharpness of hers, that clear-eyed intensity, refreshing.

She had been so very different from the other women he knew, the *safe* and *careful* women he'd chosen, and Tadeo had been mesmerized.

Kissing her was like coming home to a place he'd long since thought had burned to ash. It was an immediate shock to his system. It was like catapulting himself straight to the heart of a burning inferno and he knew better.

He knew better.

But he deepened the kiss.

Tadeo kept one hand braced on the arm of her chair and used the other to angle her jaw where he wanted it, because there was no simple kiss when it came to this. To them.

Everything with Esme was plunder, possession, and each and every time, it was perfect. She was *perfect*—

That was the word that got stuck in his head. The word that grew until it drowned everything else out, even her.

Or *almost* her.

Tadeo pulled away and found her eyes glazed, dark and starry, and her lips ripe from his. He could feel the way he wanted her like a broken bone. Like a crack and a shattering, a rending apart.

But he was a king now. There had never been any room in his life for this. There wasn't now.

"*This*," he bit out at her, though for a moment he wasn't sure that his mouth wouldn't kiss her of its own accord. That his body wouldn't mount its own rebellion, the way he could feel it wanted to in every cell. "This is the problem."

"It's not a problem," she returned, even though she was breathless. Even though she looked kissed within an inch of her life and she was round with his child but still had *lips* like that, lips that tasted like everything he'd ever wanted. "You just want it to be."

It took a Herculean effort, and he hated that it was so difficult, but Tadeo pushed himself upright and stood back. He knew that she could see exactly what she did to him. His cock was so heavy that it ached and he was certain she could see it clearly as it pressed against his trousers. He could see that greedy look in her luminous eyes. He knew what it meant.

Tadeo could also think of any number of ways that she could help him with this issue—but that was how they'd gotten into this mess.

Back in Boston. Five months ago. Every time he thought he'd found a measure of self-control, Esme proved him wrong.

Every single time.

"I don't need you to understand this," he managed to grit out, though he had to dig deep. "I don't need your comfort or your help."

"So you have said. Many times."

He hated when she used that voice, so arch and *amused* when he was stretched over quicksand and could lose his footing at any moment. Tadeo ran a hand over his face, though it did nothing to remove the taste of her from his mouth. "What you fail to understand is that I don't *want* to be the kind of man who feels the things that you make me feel, Esme."

That landed. He could see it got to her, though she covered it beautifully in an instant. Sometimes he thought he was the only one who could see behind the masks she wore. Other times he thought that the fact he could was part of this curse she'd laid on him at first sight.

And he had never found a way to stop caring when he hurt her. He never took any pleasure in it.

But it still had to be done.

"I have never wanted it," he told her, very deliberately. "Boston should never have happened. You seem to think that what happened there is the truth of things between us, but surely the past seven years should have proved to you that Boston was the aberration."

"What exactly do you think would have happened if we hadn't met in Boston?" Esme asked. She did not look as wrecked as he felt, or even as wrecked as she'd seemed for a flash a moment ago—but then, she never did. She dabbed at the corner of her mouth with a delicate finger, and shrugged. "What do you suppose it would have been like if we'd met for the first time when you decided to start courting me? How do you think that would have gone?"

He knew exactly how it would have gone. And he understood her point, though he would have preferred it if he had not.

They were conflagrations waiting to happen, the two of them. When they were together, they burst into flame. It was as simple and complicated as that.

It was entirely possible that if he'd met her for the first time on one of those public dinner dates, the whole world would have seen him toss her up against a wall and kiss her wildly, savagely, the way he had after that night in Boston.

Then, too, the whole world would have seen the way they couldn't keep their hands off each other that whole year. They would have known that he'd neglected his duties and his studies so he could spend days in bed with her, unable to do anything if it meant he had to stop touching her.

That he had even imagined himself head over heels in love.

It was the kind of alternate timeline that could keep

a man up at night. And Tadeo had already lost enough sleep over this woman.

"I know exactly what would have happened, and so do you," she said, as if she could read his mind. Sometimes he thought she could.

"I'm not debating that. The difference between us is that I know that the relationship we had—and, indeed, still have—was toxic. You seem to think it was a love story."

For the first time, he saw something in her...shake. There was a flash in her dark eyes, but more than that, he thought he saw her tremble.

A direct hit, he supposed, but he couldn't say he felt good about it. She didn't have one of her quick responses ready and he found he didn't like that either.

Esme was sitting in an ancient chair in a room noted widely for its charm and beauty, but she was the only thing he could see. She was the focal point and it was not only because she was so impractically pretty, though she was. It was because there was something about her, some lightning that crackled all over her and drew people to her.

She lit up every room she entered. She took the light with her when she left.

Leaving her was one of the hardest things he'd ever had to do. As was marrying her.

He felt like a starving man, but he took this unexpected moment of quiet between them to let himself just...*look* at her. Her lovely dark eyes that had always contained too much to bear. Too much wisdom, too much love, *too much*. Her dark brows. Those marvelous cheekbones that made her face a true work of art. That gently bowed upper lip that he dreamed about, some nights. The dark hair she wore up in the front and let cascade down behind her, a mass of thick waves.

Tadeo could smell the sweetness of her shampoo from here. The hint of coconut. The touch of spun sugar.

The woman was a menace, and that stretchy, skimpy dress she wore was not helping any.

Her breasts were indeed bigger, rounder—and now he knew why. And that rounded belly made him feel... Tadeo told himself it didn't matter what he *felt*. What mattered was how he *handled* this.

That was all that ever mattered.

"You are so afraid of this thing between us," she said, her soft voice breaking into his thoughts like a detonation.

Though he was surprised to find her gaze was directed toward the window, not at him. He thought that she was taking another swing at him, but instead, she turned her head and found him with those too-wise dark eyes once more. He thought he saw something like reproach there. Or maybe it was something deeper than that. Maybe she was simply letting him see it hurt her.

He felt his hands clench and forced himself to straighten out his fingers.

"You're terrified," Esme said, in her devastatingly quiet way, "and so you come up with all of these rules to keep it under wraps. But surely what happened five months ago should make it clear that hiding from something like this only makes it inevitable that it will burst out eventually. And now you are apparently trapped with me."

She threw all of this at him in that way she did, using

that outrageous *calm* she could pull out at will—though Tadeo knew she would probably claim that he was the one with armor.

"So what now?" she asked when he said nothing, and her dark brows rose like an indictment. "Do you shove it back down, hide it away in one of your little locked rooms, and hope for the best? Because it's been ten years now, Tadeo. The chemistry between us hasn't gotten any less intense since the day we met. In fact, I'd say it's going in the opposite direction."

He reminded himself—again—that he was the king. He had a duty to his people, one made more complicated by the damage his mother had done to the royal family's reputation. Everything he did was a restoration project, aimed at rehabilitating the family in his people's eyes—up to and including the fairy-tale wedding to the princess from the neighboring kingdom that had already been considered a love story for a quarter of a century by the time they got married.

The divorce he'd planned would have taken all of that into account.

But he wouldn't be any kind of a king—or much of a man—if he couldn't pivot when necessary.

"I've already thought of our problematic chemistry," he said.

"How shocking that you consider it *problematic*."

Tadeo should not have been pleased, somewhere down deep, that she was clearly recovered. "Seeing what you did to the Queen's Manor, a historic site that is meant to be a legacy upheld by every queen lucky enough to live there—"

"It's a house," Esme said. With excessive calm, to

his ear. "It doesn't know that it's historic. It doesn't care what color its walls are. It's amazing to me, Tadeo, that for a man so allergic to emotion, you certainly do manage to find it in the strangest places."

He wanted to jump on that. He wanted to argue. But that was what she wanted him to do, he knew that.

Instead, he stood there above her, glowering down at this bane of his existence. He knew that it had been ten years. He'd been there. But it was somehow exposing to hear her say it. Ten years of the problem that was Esme and now she was pregnant.

And he was no more in control of himself in her presence than he ever had been.

Tadeo had thought about a lot of things last night, because he hadn't slept at all. He had worked until he had to accept defeat, because he wasn't processing anything effectively and certainly not at the level he should have been. He'd gone to his private gym and had pushed himself to muscle failure as many times as he could in the hope it would put him to sleep.

But all it had done was make him tired enough that his defenses were down. It didn't do a damn thing but give him more time and space to think about this mess.

"You have spent the past seven years developing a regal persona that is, as I know you are aware, the envy of Europe," he told her now.

She gave him one of her best queenly smiles. "If I must be damned by faint praise, so be it."

He pushed on. "Instead of accepting my decision about how our marriage should operate, or even simply acknowledging that it is what *I* need whether you agree with it or not, you have always mounted this passive-aggressive campaign of yours in private."

"Oh no," Esme said, shaking her head. "I don't think that's a fair characteristic at all. I haven't been the least bit passive."

He ignored that. "What I did not realize until I saw the outrage you have visited upon the manor house is that you are as poisoned with emotion as ever. And, apparently, incapable of finding appropriate outlets—as I have."

She let out a laugh at that. "*As you have*," she repeated. "Do you have *outlets*, Tadeo? Really? Because I rather thought you shut everything off and stormed about like a computer program brought to life and in search of an algorithm."

It was the unerring accuracy that made her so dangerous, Tadeo thought. Against his will. He'd had five months as a brand-new king to consider precisely how he appeared to others—meaning, mostly, his subjects. His father had been stern, but fair.

Tadeo's team had carefully suggested that perhaps he could…*unbend*.

So, naturally, the one person alive who had ever seen him lose control—and more than once—thought he was a robot.

"This is how our marriage will work," he told her, stern himself this time. "You have often commented on the fact you felt I made all the decisions for us whether you agreed with them or not."

"I *have* commented on that," she agreed. "Because you have made all the decisions, whether I agreed with them or not. You knew that I would never back out of a betrothal that meant so much to my father. He still considers it his greatest achievement, aside from marrying my mother." Her dark eyes seemed to see too far into him. "You have shamelessly exploited the emotions you claim to find so distasteful. Is that what we're talking about? Finally?"

Tadeo ignored that aside about her family. Or tried to ignore it, anyway. It was another blow that struck too close to home. It felt a little too *right*. Was he really that shameless?

But he already knew the answer. Of course he was. He would have done anything to present the correct image of himself to his father and the world, and he had. He couldn't regret that now.

He cleared his throat. "Little as I hate to admit it, you're not wrong that pretending for all these years that this chemistry does not exist was always destined to end in an explosion. This explosion has now had consequences."

"I'm making a list now," she told him. "It will be of all the things you call our child in advance that if I hear you call them when they're here will not end well. Just so you know."

"Our lives are now irrevocably altered," he told her, and he could hear how stern and uncompromising he sounded.

Not that Esme seemed to care one bit.

"We can alter them however we see fit," she tossed back at him. Carelessly, he thought. "I know that you like to play these games of yours, where you pretend that your life is perfect, and make it look that way. But it's really not necessary. Maybe the gift you can give your kingdom is showing them that a divorce can be healthy." She shrugged. "Sometimes two people aren't meant to be together, particularly when their marriage takes place in the pressure cooker of a palace. There's nothing wrong with it. It's not shameful. I wish you could see that."

"Divorce with a child is unacceptable," he told her at once, and did not care to examine the tug deep inside him at that. As if his body rejected the very idea. "But I will also never tolerate the things my father did in his marriage."

If he'd slapped her, he doubted she would have reacted more strongly. Esme sat up straighter, her body jerking slightly, as if she really had sustained a blow. He could see color flood her cheeks.

And he didn't understand how he could feel both satisfied by that and disgusted with himself.

"Are you accusing me of something?" she asked, and for the first time in a long while, perhaps since Boston, she did not sound calm at all.

"You are clearly a woman who is ruled by her basic needs," he said. "Are you not? You always seem to be at such pains to show me that you are."

Esme shot to her feet and Tadeo thought, not for the first time, that this would all be so much easier if he wasn't so *affected* by her. Like she was in his *bloodstream*.

It was worse now. He knew that her curves were lusher and that he had done that. That was *his* baby she was carrying. *His* baby that was changing the shape of her.

Even thinking about this made him outrageously hard.

There were many things that were blurry about the

night of his father's funeral, but not the way he'd lost himself deep inside Esme. Again and again, tearing them both apart, letting himself enjoy the one indulgence he denied himself above all others.

"Will you be requiring a paternity test, then?" Esme asked sharply, her gaze dark and furious and, if he wasn't mistaken, curt. "By all means. Call in a parade of doctors. Knock yourself out and make this all about data. Maybe then you can process it."

He refused to give her the satisfaction of seeing that land. "Going forward, you will have to choose," he told her, coldly. "We are going to alter the rules of this relationship. You will, of course, take up the mantle of your responsibilities once more."

"Of course. I feel naked without my mantle, don't you?"

Tadeo decided that was simply a bid to get him to imagine her naked, which was not difficult. Or unusual. Only now he had to imagine this new, succulently *ripe* version of her and he felt himself very nearly break out in a sweat as he fought to think of anything but that.

Literally anything else.

Esme shook her head at him as if she was disappointed in him. "If you want to insult me, Tadeo, you should probably start with things that are actually possible. A slip in perfection on my part is not one of them."

He was letting her distract him, and that was another thing that needed to end. This would be a new start for them. This would, he was certain, solve a great many of their issues and make all of this *tension* dissipate.

In truth, he thought it was a brilliant solution. He

expected she would not—but he thought she'd come around.

"In private, you can either run your mouth or you can work it out in my bed," he told her starkly, and had the satisfaction of watching her mouth drop open. It was worth the wait, he thought. "You will no longer live at the manor house. You will be installed in the queen's compartments here in the palace that adjoin my own. If you cannot control your mouth, that is your choice. You will sleep in your own room. If you can manage to keep your jabs and witticisms and little veiled attacks—always delivered so archly and so *sweetly*—to yourself, like a good girl, we will work off some of this friction together."

He studied her. This time he thought the color on her face was for a different reason. "But that comes with a caveat."

"What a shock," she breathed.

"We will not discuss these things again," he told her, like thunder. "The rules are the rules. In private, you can talk all you like, but you may not touch me. Or you can touch me, but you must do so silently."

She blinked. "You can't possibly think this is healthy. This…psychotic compartmentalization. Can you?"

He moved then, responding to that part of himself he tried so hard to keep on ice, and instead of trying to lock himself down—he indulged himself.

Something he almost never did, because this fierce, overwhelming wildness surged up in him immediately. As if it only *waited* for an opportunity to burst free. It threatened to knock him over where he stood.

It was an irresistible riptide, hauling him out to sea whether he liked it or not.

Today—here—he allowed it.

Tadeo didn't fight it. He let it take him, and he closed the space between them to loop a hand around her neck. Tight enough to lift her chin up. Tight enough that he could feel the way her skin heated and her pulse went wild.

And he was close enough that he could see the look in her eyes that he both craved and tried to avoid. All that longing and need. All that glorious passion he had finally decided he could taste—but only if there were rules.

That was what he'd concluded very early this morning, after exhausting himself. He'd stood in the gallery where their wedding portrait hung—so formal and controlled—and he'd finally conceded that what had brought them here was a failure. His failure.

But he would not fail again, and that meant rethinking the boundaries that he'd maintained for the whole of his life.

"What about any of this would you call *healthy*, Esme?" he demanded, his voice unrecognizable, like a stream of smoke.

Her mouth was so close to his and he had the taste of her on his tongue already. It would be so easy—

But he could not allow it.

Tadeo had to prove to her that he could maintain the boundaries he had set out. He had to prove it to *himself*.

He made himself let go of her.

He made himself step back.

There was a kind of exultation in the pain of it—in forcing himself to do this thing he did not wish to do at all, because it was *right*. He needed the reminder.

"I suggest you take yourself back to the manor house," he told her. "And pack. Or I will instruct my staff to bring over only what I think you need."

She only stared back at him, her gaze dark and glimmering and utterly unreadable. "What a charming invitation."

"It is an order, Your Majesty," he said formally. "But you can call it what you like. Either way you will be fully installed in this palace and under my control by tonight. I suggest you start thinking about how you intend to handle it."

And then he tested himself even further. He didn't wait for her to respond. He didn't give her the opportunity to land another blow.

He turned on his heel, walked out of that salon, and left her there.

Even though every last part of him screamed for him to go back and finish what he started.

As deep and hard as possible.

CHAPTER FIVE

LEAVING THE MANOR house was painful.

Esme found herself close to tears, when really, she should have been celebrating. Steps were being taken, finally. She was moving closer to Tadeo, which was the right direction to be moving in. She knew that it was better for their baby. She hoped it would give them a chance to be…something different from this cold storage of marriage they'd been in all this time.

But it didn't matter what she *knew* or what she *hoped*. It still hurt, because this house of exile and the staff who'd helped her make it a home had been her world for seven long years. She said goodbye to each member of her staff personally. There were many hugs and promises that this would not change a thing, though Esme wasn't sure if any of them believed it.

They all knew better.

The housekeeper walked her out to her car after all the determinations had been made about what would go with Esme and what would remain at the manor house. Esme assumed that the palace would come and restore the house back to its previous elegant austerity, but she could not bear to ask about it.

"You are doing the right thing, of course, Your Majesty," the older woman said as Esme slid behind the wheel, her gaze knowing and kind. "Whether it feels like it today or not."

Esme blew out a breath. "I know that it is right. I know it."

The housekeeper nodded sagely. "At the end of the day, if I may be so bold, His Majesty the King is only a man, my lady. And sometimes they have to be *shown* things that are obvious to anyone else." She smiled. "If you'll pardon my temerity."

Esme found she held that closely to her heart over the course of the next few days. Moving into the palace required nothing of her. All she did was walk into her new bedroom and situate herself there, as part of the palace at last. As promised, her rooms adjoined the King's—but it wasn't as if that afforded them any particular intimacy.

The king's compartments took over the better part of one wing of the palace. The queen's rooms were what was left along that same wing. This was no small thing. Esme had a bedchamber, but the rest of her compartments provided her with more rooms than the manor house had.

She could wander around in them all day and not feel the least bit confined.

What made her feel as if someone had curled a fist around her were the rules. Because there were *so many* rules. Not simply Tadeo's rules, but the general palace rules too. Who could speak to whom first. When certain gestures of obeisance were to be observed, when perhaps all she wished to do was walk through the house she lived in of a morning.

It wasn't that protocol was new to her, but in the manor house, they'd all relaxed into informality. She found that reversing course was harder than expected.

Esme was grateful that moving back into the palace coincided with the resumption of her official duties. It also happened to take place during Tadeo's absence, as he was touring a new hospital complex in the far side of the country and was staying there for those days. She suspected he'd planned it that way. So that she could ease into the palace, and back into her duties, without having to worry about him in the mix as well.

Though, of course, if he *had* planned it that way, that would suggest a level of emotional intelligence that he professed not to possess.

Esme thought about what her housekeeper had said and tried to focus her energies on more important things. Like concealing her pregnancy, as it had not yet been announced widely. She hadn't even told her parents, something she felt stranger about by the day, but she had wanted to come to terms with it all first. She'd wanted to make sense of the reality of her marriage—and maybe figure out if she'd still have a marriage—before sharing the fact that she was having a child. Only her best friend, Hilary, knew, and as Hilary was a research scientist at one of the world's premier research universities, always neck-deep in her work, Esme was certain that no one else had the faintest idea.

She really had been nesting these last months.

The real truth was that she'd missed her official responsibilities. Esme quite liked the access her position gave her to people and groups that might not have found her otherwise. She liked the shaking of hands and all her interactions with the kingdom's subjects. She accepted their condolences on King Hugo's death and listened to their own stories about their feelings about the late King or their interactions with him over the years. She smiled when they told her of the hopes they held for the new King, having watched him grow up.

It was a way to connect, and Esme hoped she never took it for granted. While she felt certain that Tadeo had not brought her back to the palace to engage in any kind of healing exercise, that was what happened all the same.

And if she found herself at loose ends in the queen's compartments at night—wandering from the well-stocked library to the media room to the separate reading rooms to the salon arranged for a phantom high tea to the five different seating areas nestled here and there to the balcony that overlooked the sweep of the valley that comprised the bulk of the kingdom out toward the mountains in the distance—wondering if she really should have pushed for an escape back to America, she thought about her baby instead. She thought about the fact that whatever her relationship was or would one day become or would never be with Tadeo, it was her child's legacy that she was securing here. This was her child's birthright—this palace and everything in it, not to mention the kingdom that surrounded them. She could no more run away from that than she'd run away from her own duty, back in the day. Some responsibilities outweighed personal considerations. That was what her parents had raised her to believe, and she did.

She still did.

By the time Tadeo returned from the other side of the

kingdom, Esme felt settled in. If not *at home*, necessarily, she was comfortable. Better still, she was resolved.

Though it seemed to her that everything in the palace changed when the King was present. When he was finally *in residence* and back home. It was as if the air changed, becoming electrically charged, making everything inside the palace walls seem to *hum*.

Including her.

Even before he called her into his office the afternoon he returned, she felt that shift inside her own body. As if all her flesh and bones ever wanted to do was get ready for him, no matter what *she* might have to say about that. No matter what *she* might think was a better course of action. It was humbling.

It was also dangerous.

His office was in the public part of the palace, and the walk to reach it involved seas of glossy marble, lashings of armored statues, and kingly possessions dating back centuries. The interior of his office was a vast affair, and as stark and unwelcoming as she remembered it from before their wedding. There was the great wide desk that was kept largely empty, because the point of it was its forbidding granite massiveness. It was meant to imply that the King himself was no more tractable than the many-acred expanse of that desk of his. If the desk itself was not enough of a focal point, there were also the pieces of art on the walls, all of them grim-looking kings from throughout Bellaza's history, looking down at their descendants with what always looked like deep dismay to Esme.

Though she kept that observation to herself.

Once she was grandiosely bowed inside by his

guards, she found Tadeo already there, applying his official, slashing signature to a selection of documents in front of him. He stopped as she came in, then stood, and she offered him the curtsy that protocol demanded when she saw him for the first time in a day.

Tadeo inclined his head in return.

And then, for what felt like an intense and overlong moment, they stood there and gazed at each other.

"Does this count as mandated silence?" she asked, when the intensity felt as if it might choke her. "Since we're in your office, I assumed that this would be a work-related discussion, not something having to do with our private life. You will have to let me know."

"If it was mandated silence, you would have broken it," Tadeo replied after a simmering moment or two. "As usual."

"If you cannot explain what it is you wish me to do, I'll be forced to assume that you don't know what you wish me to do," Esme said with a shrug. "You set all this up, Tadeo. Once again, we are here in service to your wishes and your demands." Though she did smile as she said it. "I believe the onus is on you."

"You would believe this, of course," he replied in his typically chilly manner, yet always with all that brooding beneath. "As believing it suits the narrative you tell yourself."

"In any case," she said, as calmly as possible, which did not feel particularly calm today, particularly when he said such things to her, "have you given any thought about when and how you would like to make the announcement?"

Tadeo did not exactly frown, though it seemed to

suggest itself somewhere in the vicinity of his brow. "I do not think that anyone in the kingdom needs to know our precise living arrangements, Esme. Why do you?"

"I'm referring to the impending birth of your child and heir, Your Majesty," she replied, with scathing courtesy. "There will come a point—and that point will be soon—where even the most ingenious fashion in the world will not be able to hide my belly. I imagine it would be best to get out ahead of speculative articles in the press, don't you?"

His jaw flexed. She took that as a win.

"I will consult with my team and get back to you."

"Naturally," she murmured, in the same tone he'd used when discussing the *narrative* she told herself. "After all, what surely matters most when anticipating a child is the messaging."

Unsurprisingly, it turned out that words he didn't care for spoken to him in his office did indeed count against her. Though Esme found that was not a particular hardship that night, because he'd annoyed her in return.

She did not *tell herself narratives*. She was the one who had to live according to his.

"I hope it was made clear to you that you are not to treat rooms in this palace in the same shocking fashion you did the manor house," he said one evening while they were being transported to an event.

They sat in the back of one of the palace's fleets of vintage cars, each of them dressed magnificently. Her gown flowed over the seats, and while it was impossible for him not to touch the fabric, he was very careful not to touch *her*.

"No garish paint jobs, please," he told her, as if he thought she might mistake his meaning.

"No one has made anything clear to me," Esme replied sweetly. So very sweetly. "In fact, I've been under the impression that it's all been left opaque on purpose. It seems I am to be left to my own devices in all things and it is true that historically, this has indeed involved a few rounds of cheerful paints."

He sighed, and made a meal out of the sound. "Let me be the one to make certain you understand. The palace is a monument. It is the property of the kingdom as well as its joy and its emblem. Nothing in it is to be moved, renovated, changed, or even reconsidered without a consult with palace staff. Not your palace staff. Mine. Is that understood?"

"I understand perfectly," she said, in what she hoped was a voice so placid it irked him. The look he shot her way suggested that she was successful. "As there is no nursery available in my compartments, I can only hope that the royal heir will be perfectly happy to loll about on the floor. Catching every draft and building a baseline of neglect that will likely color the rest of his or her existence. When this astonishingly hardy child grows up and decides to end the monarchy in retaliation, I'm sure that his or her Spartan beginnings will figure highly in that decision."

Tadeo did not respond to that. Not with words. All he did was turn his head and fix that fulminating glare of his upon her, making it perfectly clear to Esme that if she had any designs on his body that evening, they would be denied. She had not *earned* the right to touch him. Again.

Once more, she rather thought she was glad.

But the trouble was, being irritated with him didn't last.

Too many of their engagements involved them standing too close to each other. Touching each other—whether she took his arm as they walked or allowed him to sweep her into his arms for a dance in the middle of a ballroom.

All theater, she told herself. All smoke and mirrors.

But she was weak, it turned out. It had been easier before, when she could repair to the manor house after nights like these. When she did not have to lie awake at night, knowing that he was *right there*. Right on the same hall, in the bedchamber next to hers. Sleeping beneath the same ornate roof.

And if she could only follow his obnoxious rules, she could have everything she wanted.

Everything she *thought* she wanted, that was.

For the first few weeks, she wasn't entirely certain that she did. Or maybe the real truth was that she'd always imagined that if something changed in their marriage, everything would change. It hadn't occurred to her that it could substantially change in so many respects, yet still leave her feeling as abandoned and alone as ever.

It hadn't occurred to her that there were so many more complicated places to go.

One night, Esme was so busy turning these things over and over in her head that they made it all the way to their night's engagement without her saying a word. She didn't even realize it until they were on the way home again.

It had been a long night of forced gaiety, but it turned

out that they were both quite good at that sort of thing. She'd forgotten that, somehow, over the course of the last five months. That for all that Tadeo liked to brood at her, he could turn on his charm when it mattered.

That was what she was thinking about in the car as it slipped through the old city streets and then bumped over the old cobblestones around the palace. How easy it was for him to be charming to everyone else in the world but her.

She almost asked him about it—or, perhaps, bludgeoned him a bit with it, as that was likely to make her feel better—but then she remembered.

Somehow Esme had managed, quite accidentally, to remain quiet in private this entire night.

And beside her, she was certain that she could feel Tadeo getting more and more tense the closer they got to the palace.

It was as if a light bulb went off in her head with a loud *pop*.

Esme could have kicked herself. She'd been so busy thinking about how it *felt* for her that she'd forgotten that there was no way that Tadeo would have put all these strictures into place if he wasn't trying to protect *himself* somehow too.

And now that she'd finally gotten around to thinking this through, she knew exactly how he was protecting himself with this: He didn't think she could do it.

He didn't think that she could ever stay quiet enough to win herself a place in his bed. He might even have thought, and not without reason, that the very idea that she was expected to win her place in his bed would keep her from trying. She was a Wellesley woman, after all.

It made perfect sense. Tadeo could wrap everything in ice when he had his clothes on. He could and he did.

But the moment they touched—and even more so when they were naked—he was as helpless in the face of the wildfire that they became as she was.

How could she have let herself forget this?

The car pulled up to the palace entrance. The courtiers and guards descended upon them as always to guide them inside and relay any pertinent information that could not wait to get the King's ear. But Tadeo looked over at her as they exited the vehicle.

"I want to see you tomorrow," he told her sternly. "In my office. I should like to discuss some of the finer points of protocol that I think the last five months might have erased."

Any other night, or any other time at all, Esme would have responded to that provocation in kind. But tonight she knew exactly what he was doing. And why.

So all she did was smile at him, as demurely as possible. She inclined her head graciously, wordlessly agreeing to his ridiculous demand, as if she had not been raised a princess herself and—unlike him—spent her formative years with her very own comportment instructor as her parents had not wished to send her to any finishing school. The *cheek* of the man.

But Esme said not one word.

He was pulled aside to attend to some matter or other, but Esme headed straight to her rooms. She found she was trembling, slightly, but she knew full well it was excitement. Inside her compartments, she took specific care as she went through her nightly routine. She brushed out her hair and left it to flow like ink down her back. Instead of comfortable pajamas she liked to sleep in these days, she went and dug out a chemise she'd bought before her wedding in excess of hope.

She let the silky fabric shimmer over her body and then laughed when she looked in the mirror and saw the way that her baby belly made the whole thing…shorter. And far more provocative, really.

Perfect for tonight, then.

Esme dabbed a hint of perfume at her wrists and then pressed her wrists behind her ears, because long ago, in Boston, he had once groaned about how wild that scent made him with the proof of his admiration pressed hard against her thigh.

She took a deep breath, and laughed at that too, for she felt as shaky as an untouched virgin on her wedding night. Though she had been nothing of the kind, thanks to him. And this was no wedding night anyway.

Though in a way, she thought as she walked back into her bedroom from the dressing room here that rivaled the one she'd had in the manor house, it was. This was a new beginning for them whether he liked it or not.

Because Esme was quite certain she'd finally cracked the code. Like it or not—and she was quite certain he would not like it at all, at least in theory—she'd figured him out.

She went to the door that joined their bedrooms, took a deep breath, and then pulled it open. But when she walked through, instead of finding herself in his bedchamber she discovered that she was in a small antechamber instead. It was little more than a closet, with a chair and a small table beneath a portrait of a bucolic scene that could have been any mountain slope in the

Pyrenees. A door to what was obviously Tadeo's bedroom and also a door to what she assumed was the hall.

Esme knew immediately what this room was. A little waiting area for the ladies, in case the king was otherwise occupied—as she imagined many a king had been over the course of the kingdom's long history. This room allowed His Royal and Rutting Majesty to cycle wives and mistresses in and out as he pleased without any unpleasantness that might put him off his stroke.

It was one of the things she loved about these old buildings. They always told on themselves.

But she did not intend to wait about for the King's pleasure tonight. She knew Tadeo's essential character too well, despite all these years of chilly discord shoved deep beneath their public personas. She not only knew he wouldn't be with another woman, she knew he was regretting the bargain he'd made with her, too.

Yet she also knew he kept his promises, even if that was to what he believed was his detriment.

She went to the other door, half expecting it to be locked against her.

But it opened easily when she turned the knob and she supposed that wasn't a surprise, no matter that it felt like one. Tadeo was a man of his word, good or ill.

Inside, she found herself in the King's bedchamber. It was an imposing, august sort of room. There was a grand four-poster bed on one wall and a capacious hearth with a seating area arranged around it. The rugs on the stone floor were thick and fine.

Over by the windows, bathing in the starlight, stood Tadeo himself.

She knew that he had heard her come in and she also knew, simply at a glance, that he was bracing himself against this intrusion.

He probably wanted her to say something now so that he could send her away again.

Esme would bite her tongue in half before she did anything of the kind.

Besides, she could think of far greater uses of her time. And her poor tongue. She glided across the room toward him and could see herself coming in the window's reflection. So she knew he could see her too.

He turned to face her as she came closer, no longer wearing the majestic suit with all its regalia that he'd worn out tonight. Now he wore a T-shirt and lounging trousers, yet both of them were made of a fabric so exquisite that she could see the way it fell—lovingly and caressingly—against his body from across the room.

It was even better up close. So was he.

"I don't think this is a good idea," he growled at her.

But all she did was smile at him.

Esme went up to him and stopped just before another step would send her catapulting into his body. She could feel the heat he gave off, as if he was a furnace. He smelled like the shower he must have just taken, a fragrant sort of damp that made her feel a bit damp herself.

She took a breath, because she wanted to remember every moment of this. No blurriness, no alcohol, no crushing grief—and the silence that made everything that much better. That made it all so much *hotter*.

That somehow made everything roaring here between

them as stark and undeniable as she remembered it from the night they met.

Then, holding Tadeo's gaze, Esme knelt down before him and watched those blue eyes of his burst into flame.

CHAPTER SIX

His eyes, so full of fire and need, told her everything she needed to know.

Esme knelt up and slid her palms along his powerful thighs. As she did, she could not mistake the thick impression of his cock or the way it pressed out against the soft fabric of those lounging trousers of his.

He was so big. So hard. He made her mouth water.

Still holding his gaze, she rubbed her cheek against the length of it. And listened to the telltale sign of his breath as it sighed out of him, as if against his will.

But Esme knew the sound of this man's surrender when she heard it.

Just as she knew the way it echoed inside her, making her feel shivery and magical, bright with yearning in every last cell.

She put her mouth on him, through the fabric, and smiled against him when he jerked. Though he did not push her away. She could feel the tension in him, but if anything, he pressed himself toward her mouth, not away from it.

Esme worked her way up until she could peel the waistband of his trousers down and free him at last. Then she used both of her hands to take him out of the trousers, fully. She sighed a little, happily, sitting back on her heels. She let her hands do what they liked, relearning the shape of him, the heavy weight, the bold heat.

Then she wrapped her hands around him, knelt up high again, and took him in her mouth.

She heard him groan but better yet, she could *feel* it. Then he did it again, the sound even deeper and more raw, like the fire was taking him under.

Like he was already burning alive.

And then his hands were in her hair. He took the thick length in his fists and held her head where he liked it as she licked and sucked and gave herself over to the sheer, dizzying glory of this.

To the sounds he made in the back of his throat and the hint of salt on her tongue as he surged into her mouth.

Esme could feel her whole body respond to the taste of him. To his excitement. To the delicious tension she could feel all through his long, rangy body and the fists in her hair.

She could tell the exact moment he gave himself over to her, completely. When he stopped even pretending to fight, or hold back, or keep himself apart from her in any way. When he stopped doing anything but this.

There was another raw, rough sound and then everything was sensation—so hot, so intense, so *them*—until he flooded her mouth with the essence of him.

Esme tilted her head back, swallowed him all down, and then smiled up at him. She didn't wipe away the tears that had gathered in her eyes and trekked down her cheeks, her body's usual reaction to taking him so deep in her mouth.

She was not at all surprised when his gaze went supernova and he hauled her up, straight off the floor and into his arms.

He carried her over to the bed and she thought he meant to toss her on it, but he clearly remembered that she was pregnant at the last minute. Accordingly, he *placed* her on the coverlet instead.

Esme was just pleased that he was as swept away by all this as she was tonight. More pleased than she wanted to admit, because it felt a lot less like a victory and a lot more like...something softer.

Something much more fraught with peril than beating Tadeo at his own game.

"What is this thing?" he muttered, rubbing his hands over the silk of the chemise and then pulling it up and over her head.

The look on his face when he saw her naked made her eyes go blurry.

Esme didn't know what he told himself. She didn't know how he justified all of these cold and distant years in his own mind. She only knew what he told her, but that always hinged on the official business of their royal marriage. The *messaging*. The *positioning*. The delicate math of appearances and outreach, glamour and approachability, and what the public's experience of these things meant in how they perceived the royal family.

It had all been so dry and cold for so long.

And then, of course, they'd had a wildly bright and blurry night that he had, apparently, decided he could simply write off as a mistake and never look at again before he divorced her—something he had always seemed to think he could do without too much public outcry.

The only thing he claimed to care about was what his subjects thought of him and the job he did.

If she hadn't been pregnant, Esme imagined she'd be locked up with the crisis team, working on messaging that elevated the King's desire for a divorce into a *national necessity*.

But tonight had nothing to do with any of that. It had nothing to do with any messaging or crisis management.

This was purely between the two of them. This was a culmination of the same fire that had *been* right here, between them, for a decade already and counting.

She could see it all over him. Like he'd forgotten how to be cold for a moment—just a moment. Just tonight. And instead he was something like starstruck as he took her in.

All of her.

There was a look of sheer wonder on his face as he crawled onto the bed with her and learned the new contours of her body.

The heaviness of her breasts. The new, darker color of her nipples.

The faint line from her navel down over the insistent swell of her belly.

He took the longest time there, smoothing his hands over the place where their child grew and pressing kisses all along the curve. Esme didn't know how she kept from crying.

She thought that if he knew what she could see on his face then, he would have stopped this at once. He would have thrown Esme straight out and ordered her not to return.

But he didn't know. And she wasn't about to tell him.

Instead, she kept silent—as ordered—and somehow that made everything hotter and more intense as he slid down between her legs, spread them wide, then set his mouth to the molten core of her.

Where she discovered she was even more sensitive than before.

So sensitive that she let out a shuddering sort of sound, because she was already *right there*—

Tadeo licked into her, growling the way he always had, as if her taste electrified him. As if he was enjoying himself as much as she was. He had been her first, her only. She had heard all sorts of things about what men liked and didn't like, but Tadeo had never fit into those categories.

There had never been a single part of her, or any possible activity, that he had not thrown himself into the way a person only could when they loved every moment.

Esme knew this, because it was how she felt when she got to explore his marvel of a body and make him shudder beneath her own hands.

Tonight was no different. Tadeo applied himself to the task as if he'd been dying to taste her like this for years. She threw her head back and she arched up against his mouth. She moved her hips and she gave herself over to the slow, insistent, and inexorable build of all that pleasure.

He slid one finger deep inside her, then another. And that made it better. It made everything hotter and wetter and slicker, and when he started to thrust his fingers in and out of her body, Esme simply shattered.

She bucked against him, muffling the sounds she might have made against the back of her hand.

Tadeo climbed back up the bed and lay himself out beside her, then scooped her up so that he could roll her over and arrange her above him. He settled her on her hands and knees, and it seemed the most natural and inevitable thing in the world to sit up, then guide that marvelous length of him deep inside her.

For a moment, when she sank down on him, it was like the whole world stopped spinning.

It was that glorious, that impossibly *right*, that good.

It was the same as it always was. It was perfect.

It was scalding hot and it made her want to sob out the pleasure of it, of him. He filled her completely, then slightly more, so it took her a moment to settle in against him. To let her body adjust that last small bit so that she could truly take all of him.

And this time there wasn't anything the least bit *blurry* about it.

Esme breathed until she felt herself relax internally. Even if she hadn't been able to feel it herself, she would have known by the way his gaze sharpened. Those bright blue flames.

Making her wonder if this was the time he'd cause her to simply *combust*.

After a moment, then, she propped her hands on his chest and began to work herself against him. She rocked herself back and forth. She raised herself up and then slid back down that whole, hard length of him.

He watched her, his hands on her hips to help her and to guide her, that gorgeous face of his filled with passion and command, desire and longing.

She doubted he knew she could see that, too.

Esme bit her lip and every stroke felt like glory. Like them.

Like everything she ever wanted, the way it always had.

The way it always would.

She kept on and on until his head fell back and hers drooped forward, his hands gripping her while he pounded into her from below, until they both exploded all over again—scattering themselves to every part of the Pyrenees. And the galaxy. And any universe that waited beyond.

Esme collapsed against him and he caught her, then pulled her down on top of him. She lay there, spent and giddy, especially because he didn't toss her aside the way she had assumed he might. He didn't order her to go. He didn't ruin this.

She had been so sure he would cut them back down to size that the fact he didn't made her heart swell inside her chest—until she was terrified that he would hear the way it beat. That he would know how much she loved this sweet heat they'd made and do something to make it cold again.

They lay there in the dark, silent—save for the way their breath sawed out into the dimly lit room.

And she got to drift off to sleep curled up into Tadeo's side, which was—the way it always was, the way it always had been—the best sleep of her life.

Esme wasn't exactly surprised to wake up alone the next morning. Hurt, yes. But not *surprised*.

She sat up, looking around, but she could tell immediately that he was nowhere nearby. That wasn't surprising either.

And when the immediate hurt subsided, she decided

that she was perfectly satisfied. She had seen his face. She had held his body close to hers, and held him inside her. And yes, all of those things were true about the night of his father's funeral, too.

She remembered that night entirely too well, despite the alcohol. She had found him in his father's study, down near the offices in one of the more public areas of the palace. He had disappeared after the funeral and she hadn't wanted to just…leave him to his grief.

Maybe it was silly, after all they'd been through over the years, but she couldn't bear to think of him hurting. She'd instinctively headed for the study, not sure if she knew or simply remembered that his father had spent the bulk of his time with his books in his last years.

Sure enough, she'd found Tadeo there. Systematically working himself through a very large bottle of something amber-colored and pungent.

I don't want you here, he'd growled at her when she'd come in, dressed in her fine black clothes.

But he'd gestured to the couch beside him, inviting her to take a seat.

Esme hadn't intended for things to go the way they had. Or she didn't think that was what she'd intended. They hadn't spoken much. He'd passed the bottle to her and they'd traded back and forth like that for far longer than they should have.

When he'd buried his head in his hands, she'd rubbed his back—and then it had seemed like the most natural thing in the world when he'd pulled her close and kissed her.

It had been a savage kind of grief, she thought. She

had offered him comfort, because she knew he needed it. Because she'd known and cared about his father. Because despite everything, she cared about him, too.

Maybe that was when she'd understood that she always would.

But it had been followed by that slow-dawning understanding that, once again, he was going to pretend none of it had happened. He was going to pretend it had been a forgettable drunken night.

He was going to carry on exactly as he always had.

Esme had been forced to go through the painful process of finally—finally—accepting that her life with him was over. That there was no future. That no matter how many times he'd once told her he loved her, safe across an ocean from here, or how often she thought that really, he still did, it didn't matter.

He didn't want to. And he would act as if he didn't into the grave.

She'd finally accepted that she really and truly couldn't change him. That this was a doomed enterprise, it was time to cut her losses, and she'd be better off out there without him.

Esme had started imagining what that might look like. She'd been, if not *excited*, ready.

But now, sitting in his bedchamber all alone, Esme understood that she'd been lying to herself. She didn't simply *care* about Tadeo. She hadn't really accepted that he didn't love her the way she wanted him to—she'd simply accepted the fact that it was going to end and there was nothing she could do about it.

She had been head over heels in love with him since

the moment she'd laid eyes on him in that Boston restaurant ten years ago.

Nothing had ever changed that love. Not the way he'd ripped her heart out of her chest a year after that first meeting. Not the way he stomped on what was left of it repeatedly during their agonizingly public—and so deeply fake—courtship. Not the way he'd broken the remaining pieces beyond repair at their cold, heartless wedding.

Not the past seven years of cold duty and quiet exile.

Not even her own acceptance that it was far past time to stop pretending that it could ever be something he wouldn't allow it to become.

Not even now, pregnant with his child, naked in his bed, alone.

Esme had loved him all along. She loved him still.

A big breath seemed to come from deep inside her then, not sure if it was a sigh or a sob. She took that as a sign to go. She got up from the bed and looked around for her chemise, but couldn't find it anywhere.

The palace was not the place to be wandering around naked—that was surely against protocol—so she pulled the coverlet from his bed, wrapped it around herself, then made her way back through the antechamber that happily did not contain a mistress and into her own bedroom. It was set up very much like his was, though her four-poster had a canopy and her fireplace had a mantel festooned with lovely objects that she could tell at a glance were priceless.

She went and sat in front of the fire, though it wasn't lit. She stared into the cold hearth.

"I love him," she whispered into the uncaring bedchamber around her that must have heard too many confessions to count. Maybe she'd accepted that she always would, but she wasn't sure if she'd really understood, until this moment, that she had never really intended to divorce him no matter what daydreams she'd let herself have about other lives without him.

Because surely she could have divorced him herself at any time if she'd truly been ready to leave him. In fact, she could have changed the course of their relationship at any time, but she never had.

She could have declined his courtship. Her parents would not have forced her. Esme liked to bang on about responsibility, pandering to her people, and giving them what they wanted. But was that really what she'd done?

Or was this what she'd wanted all along—to be near him, no matter how?

Because she might not have him the way she wanted him, but she had him just the same.

Esme knew he hadn't touched another woman in the time they'd been married. He'd told her that much, drunkenly, the night of his father's funeral.

Now, all she could think was that it was a shame. All those years of celibacy for both of them, and for what?

When they could have been doing this the whole time. Though he wouldn't want that, she knew. Because Tadeo liked to play his games, but he couldn't keep his distance from her when sex was involved.

He'd proved that back in Boston in that house of his in Beacon Hill.

The truth was that it had never been *sex* between

them. It had never been as simple as a *release*, or *a little bit of fun*, or whatever people liked to claim sex was—or should be—these days. These were conversations that made Esme think the people having them had never had the kind of sex that she and Tadeo did.

Life-altering. Earth-shattering. Absolutely catastrophic in all the best ways, and maybe in some not-so-great ways, too.

But there was no pretending that the things they did to each other didn't change them both. Even Tadeo had never denied that. *I love you*, he would whisper while he was deep inside her, his hands in her hair and his mouth against her cheek, her neck, her mouth. *I love you, Esme*, he would murmur as they drifted off to sleep, fused together like some kind of Gordian knot. He had denied he'd said those things, but never the passion that had prompted him to say them. His contention was always that the kind of passion that ignited between them was a liability and he could not allow it to derail his monarchy.

She blew out a breath and pulled that coverlet tight around her. As she did, she accepted another truth she wasn't sure she wanted to sit with.

Esme didn't want to divorce him. She didn't want to raise their baby in this environment of cold distance and responsibility and no love.

She wanted everything. The mess, the passion, the *hurt* of it all. The love that had changed them both so profoundly. The love that they both deserved.

A *husband*, not an officemate.

Her man, not just a king.

And it was also true that she had no idea how she was going to go about getting it, but Esme knew one thing.

Last night had been an excellent start.

CHAPTER SEVEN

As the days passed and the nights continued to set them both afire, Tadeo came to the careful, considered conclusion that everything was going well.

Or as well as could be expected.

It had been a bit of a rocky start to this new phase in their marriage, he could admit. Possibly only rocky for him, little as he liked to imagine himself so affected, but the reality was that Esme seemed as unaffected as ever. As if she had only been waiting for the opportunity to have something far closer to a real marriage and was happy to dive straight in.

As if she was less thrown by the uncontrollable wildfire that still burned between them. As if she *liked* it.

He could not allow himself to think about *how much* she liked it when he was attending to his many duties during the day. And yet, too often, he could think of nothing else.

The first night that Esme had come to his room had thrown him. He hadn't expected that she would ever manage to keep her mouth shut. He had never known her to try. The girl he'd met in Boston had been a revelation. She had shared her ideas, her dreams, her theories, her opinions, her questions, her silliness—all seemingly without a shred of concern that she might be judged for these things.

Indeed, Tadeo had not judged her. He'd been too smitten with her.

Esme had burst into his life and shown him all the light and possibility that he'd been raised to abhor, because his father was a man of neither too few nor too many words. King Hugo prided himself on always being concise. Precise.

Pointed.

And he never spoke simply to fill a space.

Tadeo had aspired to be just like him.

Meanwhile, Esme's words could fill rooms and paint them too, in all the vibrant colors she held inside her. Sometimes, in the long years of this cold marriage, he had found himself awake when he ought to have been sleeping—imagining what it looked like inside her head. How bright it must be in there.

How different from this kingdom of icy winters and cool summers, and the deep freeze he kept himself in. Even if it was by choice.

This was why he'd been so certain that the deal he'd made with her favored him. He had never known her to stay quiet for too long. Not even when she should have.

He'd convinced himself she would never manage it. That she would be too busy finding new and clever ways to eviscerate him with her tongue to ever follow the rules that would lead her to his bed. That she might *try* to make it happen, but would fail at the slightest provocation.

That she hadn't made him wonder if he knew her as well as he'd always assumed he did.

She had fallen asleep in his arms and he held her there, liking the sensation entirely too much. He stared at the ceiling, wondering if he'd made a terrible mistake.

Again.

But as the night went on, he decided that he could handle this. He could handle their chemistry as long as it was confined to the spaces where it belonged and could thus be contained. What he could not allow was it bleeding over into everything else. He was not a graduate student any longer. He could not be so reckless this time. He was a king and he had a whole kingdom to consider. He could not let passion make everything *blur*.

Tadeo decided that he could do it, and more, that this was a natural and reasonable evolution in their marriage— providing he maintained the strictest control outside the bedroom. They were husband and wife. Their marriage looked like the fairy tale they'd crafted it to be to please the outside world. He already knew she was an excellent queen in all the ways that mattered to the kingdom.

There was no reason why she couldn't make him a kind of wife that he wanted, too, sex included. It had been so long since Boston now. It was all less raw.

He knew better than to let his feelings trick his tongue into admissions that might ruin him.

As long as he maintained the strict control of his emotions that he'd held in place since breaking up with her back then—and they were second nature to him now, a part of who he was, as automatic as breathing—Tadeo couldn't see why it would be a problem.

And besides, Esme could not help but be who she

was. That meant she could not always control her mouth and some nights, he was quite certain she didn't even bother to try.

"Our presence is requested at the wedding of King Gervais," he told her one afternoon, as they sat in his office discussing their schedules—one of the anodyne diary meetings he insisted upon. Not because he could not have had access to her schedule either way, but because he liked to test himself in her presence.

"King Gervais has been married two times before," Esme pointed out.

"And the heads of all the houses of Europe have been invited every time," Tadeo replied. "This is no different. We will, of course, make our appearance."

Esme studied him. The rules of their arrangement had evolved over the past weeks. If the discussion was purely related to the business of their responsibilities, that did not count against her. It did not mean she lost her chance to find him in the night.

If, however, she got emotional about anything—by his reckoning, not hers—it did.

She kept studying him now and Tadeo felt his pulse pick up, because he knew that look in her dark eyes. It was Esme's version of *devil-may-care*. The point at which he could almost see her throw up her hands and say, *what the hell*, though she would never be *quite* so vulgar.

Or not in front of him, anyway.

"Have you met King Gervais's intended?" Esme asked. Calmly.

Too calmly, by his reckoning. The kind of calm that typically foretold an explosion, if he was not mistaken.

"I have."

"I haven't," Esme murmured, toying with the hem of the sweater she wore over a dress that made her look entirely too pretty and also—through the magic of fashion he could not begin to parse—not particularly pregnant. "But I am certain I can list the accomplishments that allowed her to rise to King Gervais's notice." If she saw the reproving look on Tadeo's face, she ignored it. "Let me guess, she is significantly younger than him, *spectacularly* more beautiful than him, and, most importantly, sheltered and naive in every possible way."

"She is an heiress of no small means from Brazil," Tadeo said. Carefully. "I believe she was selected because she meets all of the King's needs."

Those needs, in Gervais's case, did not involve dynastic aspirations as his first wife had already provided the throne with its next in line and two spares—along with scathing critiques in the press. Those needs did not involve the old king's much-discussed heart, as he had already made a fool of himself over his second wife, a wholly unsuitable actress, who had left him for her personal trainer.

Gervais had cannily selected a new queen who would give him no trouble at all.

Tadeo dreamed of such a queen.

As if she could read his mind, Esme smiled. Tadeo knew immediately, before she said a word, that he'd won today. Though was it really winning when it meant he would not have access to her tonight? Who was he punishing?

But that was a question for another time.

"You kings and your perfect little heiresses," Esme

said, in a perfectly pleasant tone that was at complete odds with that sharp look in her eyes. "It's like a sweet shop, is it not? Shiny, brightly colored, consumable objects for you to eat up and throw away. How lovely for them."

He should have ignored this entire line of conversation. And he should not have felt the least bit as if she'd landed a blow. "What you seem to forget, Esme, is that you were raised to be the same sort of bit of candy."

"Incorrect," she retorted, and he thought she sat a little straighter. More, there seemed to be something almost *condemning* in the way she looked at him. Or maybe it was worse than that. Maybe she looked *disappointed*. "I am my father's heir, as you know perfectly well. It was his dearest wish that I married you so that our neighboring nations could once again unite the way they did long ago in antiquity. If not as one nation, then as the closest of friends and allies. Our first child is meant to rule Bellaza, our second, Clarebonne." Esme tilted her head to one side. "Surely you have not forgotten this."

He had not forgotten it so much as he had never imagined that it would matter, as he'd never intended to touch her again. But something kept him from saying that.

She continued. "I was never intended to be an object on a shelf, sat there to be admired from afar. I am expected to instruct the heir to Clarebonne in the ways of the kingdom in the same manner that I was instructed myself. You know that."

He shifted uncomfortably in his chair and blamed her for it. "I remember your father mentioning that, yes."

In truth, he remembered that her father had spoken

for some time about his dreams for grandchildren and the unification of their kingdoms, but Tadeo had not bothered to pay close attention. So sure had he been that such a future would never materialize.

Esme studied him in that same way, and he could not account for how deeply he disliked it. It seemed as if she could see *into* him. "I can only assume that you're trying to be provocative, then. Does it make you feel as if you've won something?"

He disliked *that* even more.

"It's not my fault that you can't either school yourself from your emotional outbursts or simply keep them to yourself," he said, proud that he sounded very nearly disinterested. As if she was a science project he was observing from afar. "Sometimes you can, of course. What that tells me is that you are making a choice. You could choose something else, Esme." He could see it so clearly. They could be models of cool propriety and exquisite protocol by day and keep the rest of it purely in the bedroom. Expressed only and over that one way. "Everything could change for the better, and for good, if you would only obey."

She leaned in, and he was struck by how much rounder she was now and how well her dress hid it. He found he hated that it was hidden. It continued to surprise him, how beautifully her pregnancy suited her. As if she was made to bear children.

He didn't know what it was about that notion—about her ripeness and her round sweetness—that made him feel as if he was breaking his own rules. As if that was an emotional thing he was feeling rather than a simple observation.

"You would hate it if I obeyed," Esme told him, with a laugh. "You would be bored out of your mind."

Tadeo could not have said why that infuriated him. "I rather doubt that."

"You would calcify in real time, Tadeo, and do you want to know how I know that?" She didn't wait for him to answer. "Because you were a shell of yourself for seven years. And *I* was perfectly fine."

"You were creeping about the manor house like a hysteric in an asylum," he shot back. "Smearing paint on the walls and befriending your servants. I would argue that you were something very far indeed from *fine*."

And the name she called him then—in her cool, crisp, *calm* way—was so outrageous that he decided she'd lost access to him for a week.

He told himself that his reaction was the only possible one to have. That he was doing the right thing and she was testing boundaries that he needed to uphold.

But he also knew that it was the loneliest week he'd had in a long while.

He was happier than he wished to admit when it ended and she managed to bite her tongue in the face of his pointed provocation after a dinner with some ministers, allowing him to glut himself in her once more.

Afterward, they lay together. Tadeo traced patterns against her belly, murmuring to the child inside. A habit he chose not to question himself about overmuch. All he knew was that he no longer thought of the child they were having as a problem, or any of the other things he'd called this pregnancy when he'd first heard of it.

These nights with her, with the baby a very real presence between them and with them, had changed everything for him.

He could not think of the last time he'd thought of this child as anything but that. *His child.*

Something of a marvel, if he was honest. He didn't think that strayed *too* far over the line into maudlin.

"I saw the palace physician again today," she said. He already knew this. But he had not expected her to share it and he found that his chest felt unexpectedly tight when she did—and of her own volition. Another marvel, perhaps. "Do you want me to tell you what we're having? A boy or a girl?"

He knew the answer to that too. But he nodded, to let her tell him.

"A boy," she said softly. Almost shyly, he thought. "And I wondered if one of his names should be Hugo, to honor your father. And the night he was made."

Tadeo felt too many things slam into him then. They all seemed to crash around inside him, when he would have said he was immune. He would have said that he wasn't the sort of man who felt anything, because that was the kind of man he wished to be.

But he felt *this*. He felt all of *this*. Too much of *this* to name.

The trick, he decided, was in not showing it. Ever. In keeping it contained. "I'd like that," he managed to grit out.

Then he kissed her, hot and hard, to forestall any further conversation.

She was six months pregnant now. Time was running out. Soon, their child would be here and Tadeo found that he both couldn't wait—and couldn't imagine what that would be like. His own memories of childhood were divided between the happier, brighter memories from before his mother died—mostly of her laughter, the games she would play with him, and the way they'd sometimes hidden from his father. In those memories, he recalled only shadows and glimpses of his father, as if he was more a monster from a nightmare instead of simply part of a game.

His later memories were sadder and quieter, as he'd learned the truth about all those bright memories of Queen Marisol and how truly noble and good his father had always been in the face of her sins. So there was regret laced through it all too, that he'd been too young and foolish to understand what was happening.

This was not something he shared with anyone. He could still remember—too well—when he'd said something along those lines to Esme in Boston.

They had been wrapped up in each other in his bedroom in the house he'd bought for his studies in the leafy, gaslit, cobblestoned neighborhood that had reminded him of home. *I wish I could have seen my mother for who she was while she was alive*, he'd said in an unguarded moment.

It chilled his blood to remember himself like that. So *open*. So *vulnerable*.

Esme had propped herself up on her elbow and pushed the weight of her hair back from her face. She'd looked at him seriously. Too seriously. *You saw your mother as your mother. Maybe that's a gift.*

Tadeo did not like to think about how often those words came back to him. How they'd haunted him across the years. He hated that he'd allowed that moment to happen, but he'd hated even more that he couldn't let it go.

The next day he found himself in the portrait gallery, studying the formal portrait that hung beside his and Esme's. It was of his parents in their wedding finery and Tadeo wasn't sure why it had never occurred to him that his parents might very well have been as at odds with each other while they'd sat for theirs as he and Esme had been.

That maybe there had never been the happy period he'd liked to think there had been. Maybe that had been a story they told. An act they put on.

He certainly knew how that went.

Tadeo found himself looking at his own wedding portrait. It was so cold, he thought now. They looked like strangers who happened to have found themselves in the same ornate frame, subject to the same brushstrokes with nothing else in common.

Though he would not have described it like that before his father's funeral had turned everything on its head. Back before that fateful night, he would have said that he and Esme looked formal, yes. Perfectly appropriate. She sat in her lovely gown and he stood behind her in the usual pose for a portrait like this.

Two people who looked suitably solemn as they started their life of duty and obligation together, he'd thought.

Now Tadeo thought he looked distant and faintly disapproving. And while Esme looked beautiful, as always, if he was fully honest with himself, she also looked terribly sad.

What he didn't like was that his parents looked much the same to him now.

Tadeo didn't think of his mother as *sad*. Careless, certainly. Reckless and scandalous, but not *sad*.

Somehow, the fact that he was having a son—within a few months—brought this home to him. He found himself thinking about his parents more than he had in a long while, and in ways that felt different to him. He particularly found himself thinking about that expression on his mother's face.

Had she truly been *sad*? And if so, why had his father not done something about it?

That felt disloyal. He hated that he could entertain any notion that did not paint his father in the bright light King Hugo deserved.

"And to what end?" he asked himself during one of his ferocious workouts on a night that Esme had decided to poke at him, thereby ensuring he would sleep alone.

He lifted weights until he thought his muscles would betray him and then he walked back toward his rooms, not pleased when his mind took him back again to his father.

But not about his mother this time.

What was on Tadeo's mind tonight was his child. His soon-to-be-born baby. He preferred the nights when Esme followed the rules—that he relaxed once she was there, he acknowledged, because they talked in bed now. He preferred sleeping with her, yes, for all the expected reasons and more. But he also liked that he had access to his baby.

He could not conceive of treating his child as anything but the miracle he was. He already liked to feel him kick and roll. The child wasn't here yet and his antics already made Esme laugh and even Tadeo smile in the cocoon of his bed.

He could not imagine how he would take these feelings within him and turn them off. The truth of the matter was that when it came to his son, Tadeo did not feel neutral or icy at all.

What he could not figure out was why—or, crucially, *how*—his father ever had.

CHAPTER EIGHT

The wedding of King Gervais and his young and starry-eyed heiress took place in the former's kingdom in its iconic cathedral that was mostly famous for having not been bombed in any of the twentieth century's wars.

Esme and Tadeo entered the cathedral with all the rest of Europe's royals and nobles, all of them walking across the grand forecourt in their finery while looking pleasantly sophisticated for the cameras and the crowd.

In many ways, Esme thought as they walked in the sedate procession, this was something of an extended family reunion. The grand crowns of Europe had been intermingling for so many centuries that it was likely more difficult to find two royal families that *weren't* related to some degree. Somewhere in their gilded family trees.

They were directed to their seats, where there was a great deal of nodding and smiling, even between heads of state who would normally consider themselves enemies. Weddings called for better manners. Or at least a competition to see who could pretend better.

Esme knew her ability to seem delighted in her surroundings, no matter what, was top-tier. And despite his penchant for chilliness, Tadeo could do the same.

Still, it was a relief when the ceremony started in all its high pageantry, and the graciousness no longer had to be directed at each other. Everyone could relax and watch an old king marry a young woman as if it was still medieval times.

A sentiment Esme rather thought she could see on almost every face in the cathedral. Especially the faces of Gervais's heirs.

Esme had been to a friend's wedding some while ago on a beach somewhere along the rugged Maine coast. The officiant had gotten certified online. The bride and groom had made up their own vows and the whole thing had been interrupted by some chattering seagulls.

It was amusing to sit in the middle of a spectacle like this one and think about ceremonies like that. So unpretentious. So easily accessible. The entire wedding party and all the guests had fit into one small dining area in a nearby pub. It had been lovely.

This was not that kind of wedding.

After the ceremony, there was another procession out of the cathedral. It was another opportunity for Europe's aristocracy to wave at the cameras and the gathered crowds as they slipped into a sea of waiting Rolls-Royces and were borne back to the palace.

"These weddings are all the same," Esme said when they were settled in their car, her mouth fixed in a cheerful smile as she waved to the crowds outside the window. "It could have been our wedding. The only thing that changes are the coats of arms and the languages."

"It is yet one more way that monarchies remain eternal." From beside her, Tadeo was offering a wave of his own out the opposite window. "How else would anyone know to support us?"

Esme looked over at him. "That sounded suspiciously like republican sentiment dressed up in sardonic inflection."

"Perish the thought." But he glanced over at her. "Though I will say that it is...*different* to know that I am bringing a child into this world. Into this pressure. I would not change my life in any regard." Esme thought he put a little too much emphasis on the word *any*. Then was surprised when he kept going. "But I can't deny it had its challenges."

Esme rested her hands on the convenient shelf of her baby bump, no longer hidden at all today. It had been decided that they might as well use this opportunity to launch her pregnancy to the world in one go. *Not a moment too soon*, Esme had thought when the team had informed her of this decision, because she couldn't imagine that very many people had been fooled this whole time no matter what games she'd played with shapes and fabric and flow.

Still, back home in their own kingdom, the people would only whisper their suspicions. They would not print them, out of respect.

There was nothing respectful about the broader European tabloid press, and so Tadeo's team had decided that they would use the expected feeding frenzy to their advantage. The thinking was that the tabloids could and would shriek about Esme's Royal Bump or some such thing and then cooler heads from the palace would put out a far more restrained announcement. The kingdom would tut at the intrusiveness of the press and would in fact argue that *were it up to them, they* would not wish to know if the Queen was pregnant until *the day she gave birth*.

Even now, pictures of her in her wedding finery that had been altered to showcase her belly should likely be appearing on all the usual websites. It was all part of the game, and few people played the game better than Tadeo and his message-obsessed public relations team.

But it also felt like a good thing, Esme thought as the car inched along the ancient streets of this old, storied European city. She might not have wanted her marriage to have been the way it was for those first seven years. She might not have wanted the divorce she knew that Tadeo had been so bent upon, either, though she'd been prepared for it.

She was well aware that this baby was the reason everything had changed. It was possible that there was a part of her that resented it, but it was a vanishingly small part of her. If that. Because she had always wanted Tadeo more than she'd ever wanted to be free.

The reveal of her pregnancy meant that he was accepting their future too. She couldn't hate that.

Esme knew that Tadeo believed that *he* decided whether he got to feel emotion, and hated that she had always forced him to do exactly that and not on his schedule. She didn't know how to tell him that a baby was likely to do the same—babies being babies—but that didn't matter. He would find out soon enough, and anyway, the great thing about their marriage was that there were dynastic implications to the children they had. The only option he'd had to get rid of her was to make sure there was no issue. That was the only way he might have managed to pull off the supposedly amicable split she assumed he'd wanted to sell to his people.

The whole world would have assumed—no matter what they said—that the marriage had ended because she couldn't have children. Whether they thought that was sad or not, they would have accepted that as a fair reason for a king to find a new wife.

Just in case Esme liked to pretend that the world had moved on from the Dark Ages.

Oh well, she thought now. *That won't be happening now.*

But these were not the challenges Tadeo was talking about.

"I think that we are uniquely qualified to mitigate the challenges of this life," she said, her belly warm beneath her palms. "My parents very much wanted me to have more real-world experiences than some other heirs to thrones. I went to grammar school with the public. That was very important to them. I did go to a private school after that, but they insisted that I leave the country for college, so I could see something of the world outside of Clarebonne. They were deeply opposed to those finishing schools so many queens are polished up in. I think they always felt strongly that education was by far the better thing to concentrate on when manners can always be learned."

"I'm not sure that schooling is the issue," Tadeo said.

Esme smiled. "Is it not? Where else will you interact with others who are not of your rank? Who do not share your history? I think schooling is very important. Not just for the education you might receive, but for the social interaction. How else can you get to know your subjects?"

Tadeo looked as close to *bewildered* as she'd ever seen him. "My father had a different view of the situation," he said after a moment. Then he cleared his throat. "He spoke to me of duty, of course. And the responsibilities that would always trump any of my personal concerns, naturally. But when it came to education, he was very traditional." He named the famous boarding school he'd attended that was known to handle the schooling of a great many royal children, not to mention the offspring of celebrities and billionaires of all stripes. "Then Cambridge, of course. Followed by Harvard, as you know. My father considered this a sort of hat trick of an educational pedigree."

"But you already had a pedigree," Esme pointed out softly. "The child I'm carrying does too."

She thought that he looked taken back. Or, again, something like *bewildered*—though he hid it quickly beneath his more typical neutral expression. He aimed his attention out the window again, to continue the smiling and waving that was expected in situations like this.

"These are things I'm sure we can argue about once a child is here," he said, dismissively. But it was like those nights when she was obediently silent and he started poking at her. She had the distinct impression that he was trying to get her temper to flare. He wanted her to fight with him, clearly.

Esme looked out the window again, but she didn't see the crowds pressing in at the barricades. She had a little prickle of awareness that told her that this was an important moment, so she couldn't quite see why. Aside from her inkling that he wanted her to poke back at him, he was perfectly right. They had years to worry about the schooling of their unborn child, not to mention what sort of society the next king might keep.

But somehow it felt as if this was a bruise that she'd unknowingly pressed against.

At the palace there were more cameras, and she could already hear the roars from the paparazzi as Tadeo helped her from the car. He made certain to pause for a moment outside it, as if he needed to adjust his sleeves, with her belly on full display. Then there was the long procession up the palace stairs and in through its grand gates that allowed most of Europe to get a glimpse of the contours of her pregnancy.

Precisely as planned, she knew. Esme couldn't quite put her finger on why it was that she felt so unsettled by the conversation they'd had in the car.

It wasn't his rules. As the weeks passed, they had loosened. Now it was not pure silence that he required. It was pleasantness. Only if he felt attacked, or he felt she was being unreasonable, did he decree that she'd lost access to him.

Though it was never for a week these days and the real truth was, he didn't do that much anymore anyway. It was as if he'd become as addicted to their nights together as she was. Esme suspected that he didn't sleep any better without her than she did without him.

But she didn't dare say that, either.

What she did instead was pour her feelings into everything they did. Whether it was a dance at a ball or the way she held on to him as she found her pleasure, she did anything and everything she could to infuse these moments with the love she felt swimming inside her, as sure as the blood in her veins.

Sometimes she was sure that he could feel it. Sometimes, in those unguarded moments when they were together and naked, and there was nothing in all the world but the fire they built together, she was sure that she glimpsed it. That light in his eyes. When he looked at her, sometimes, that curve in his mouth.

All those things he never said.

Inside the palace, they moved along a gorgeous entry hall that led into a ballroom. They were announced and then they walked down the stairs and were swallowed up by the crowd. Only then did Esme allow herself to start looking around with purpose.

"Are you expecting to meet someone here?" Tadeo asked, sounding amused.

"My parents." She smiled up at him. "They are the King and Queen of Clarebonne, after all. I feel certain they are on the guest list."

"They didn't tell you?" He looked confused.

"Why would they tell me?" She shook her head at him, though she didn't think he was joking. "Gone are the days when the Clarebonne palace kept me apprised of the King and Queen's movements."

"I thought you said you spoke to your mother every day."

"I do." Esme frowned at him. "We don't talk about work, generally."

Again, Tadeo looked as if he couldn't quite comprehend what she was saying. "Then what do you talk about?"

Esme didn't get a chance to answer him, because he

was swept into conversation with some other heads of state. But she couldn't stop thinking about what that question revealed. About what it suggested about his relationships with his parents. With his father, most of all.

Had they ever *not* talked about work?

She moved through the grand ballroom, smiling and clasping hands with many of the people she recognized as she went. And she recognized almost everyone. It was all quite lovely, and in some cases decidedly not lovely—that was part of the fun of these events, she always thought—and either way, she found herself smiling far more genuinely when she saw the people she was looking for standing over near an alcove.

Her mother saw her a few moments later as she drew near, and Queen Luisa's practiced, regal smile turned into something far more personal, wide and happy, at the sight of her daughter.

Then her gaze dropped to Esme's belly and her smile dropped. It became a gasp. Then she tugged on her husband's arm in a complete violation of all known protocol, yanking his attention away from the earnest Dutch minister he was speaking with.

And when Esme finally reached them, they were both talking a mile a minute, hugging her close and already making noises at her baby belly. Then even more noises when she told them it was a boy.

For a while, there was nothing but that. This outpouring of emotion, so pure and so happy, that it took Esme a few extra moments to realize how much she'd missed it.

How inured she'd become to the empty shell of Bellaza. And her less empty, but still decidedly cold husband—

But that made her heart hurt all over again, and she didn't want to *hurt*. Not now. Not while her parents were here and felt like a long dose of sunlight after an endless winter.

"You have been holding out on us," her father, King Alain, said sternly, though his dark eyes danced.

"I have been," Esme confessed.

"I'm sure she had her reasons," said her mother at once, because Queen Luisa never had and never would waste an opportunity to champion her daughter. No matter what.

Tonight, Esme couldn't help but wonder who had ever championed Tadeo.

That made her heart ache too.

When her father's attention was reclaimed by the Dutch minister, Luisa linked her arm through Esme's and hugged her close.

"I'm so happy for you, my darling," she said in her musical way. "But at such a happy time, what I cannot understand is why your eyes are so sad."

Esme felt all her breath go out of her in a rush. She felt both exposed and seen, her mother's specialty. It felt like a kind of nostalgia. Like a perfect hug she knew would end. "Not *sad*," she said after a moment, when she was sure her voice would not sound the least bit rough or choked. "It's more complicated than that."

Queen Luisa studied her daughter for a moment, then turned her attention to the crowd before them. She kept her arm linked with Esme's as her own gaze took on a faraway look.

"You know that Queen Marisol and I were friends, do you not?" But that was not really a question, Esme knew. This was a story. And that she'd invoked the name of the scandalous Marisol, the much-maligned mother of Tadeo, had Esme immediately riveted. "Long before she was the Queen of Bellaza, she was a childhood friend. We grew up together, I suppose you could say, and spent several summers in our youth doing the same circuit of house parties with the sorts of people our parents wanted us to know, outside of the glare of the headlines." Her smile was mysterious, but all she said was, "I got to know her rather well."

"No one speaks of her in the palace," Esme said softly.

Her mother made a low noise. "I am not surprised."

"When she does come up, it is never a pleasant conversation."

Luisa made a humming sort of noise. Esme knew that sound. It was her elegant way or dissenting without succumbing to a vulgar snort or a laugh.

"I will tell you this," her mother said. "The Marisol I knew was a bright light. She was always happy while the rest of us liked to waft about complaining of our boredom and disaffection, as you do. She could make the most tedious afternoon a delight, simply by her presence. And when she fell in love with Hugo of Bellaza, it seemed at first that he made her the happiest she'd ever been."

Esme looked at her in surprise and her mother nodded. "It was not long after their engagement, I think, that she started to change. She grew quieter. More careful. After a while, there was no sign of the childhood friend I'd known for so long. She had become Queen Marisol." Luisa looked at Esme then. "And Queen Marisol was the saddest woman I have ever known."

Esme felt something like an earthquake deep inside her.

"Mother," she said, shaking her head. "I'm having his baby—"

Luisa's eyes flashed. "And you owe that baby *you*, Esme. My daughter is a bright light herself. Yet every time I see you, the light grows darker and darker in your gaze. Is this what you wish to pass on to your child?" She made a soft noise. "I would tell you that Marisol most assuredly did *not* want that. Yet that is where she ended up. And if I'm not mistaken, the child she loved to distraction takes after his father. Not her. Not the parent who loved him because he was hers, not because he would one day be king."

Then the music changed and they were interrupted by distant cousins. Luisa squeezed Esme's arm with her own, kissed her on the cheek, then let her go.

And Esme found herself thinking of nothing else but what her mother had said for the rest of the evening. She kept her professional smile in place. She applauded the bride, who looked like she thought she'd won the Cinderella lottery. She smiled at the groom, who looked very pleased with himself. She danced more than once with her husband, who she'd once thought would be her own fairy tale, and tried her best to get the sadness out of her eyes.

Whatever her mother had seen. Whatever that meant.

That night, they stayed in a fine old house near the palace, and made love to each other with a ferocity and a depth that made Esme think she might actually weep.

Particularly afterward, where she laid curled up beside him, and had to accept that whatever she thought was happening, it was a certainty that *he* did not think making love as part of what they were doing. *He* could be telling himself anything.

He might not even find all of this as beautiful and transformative as she did.

"Are you all right?" he asked in the dark, the two of them so close on the new bed. "You seem…"

But he didn't finish what he'd been about to say. He kissed her instead. He threw them straight back into that fire of theirs.

Hadn't he made it clear? He didn't *want* to hear the things she had to say. He didn't *want* to listen to her, because when he did, he had to *feel*.

Esme couldn't seem to get that out of her head. They flew back to Bellaza and she told herself that her spirits should have been lifted as they descended down into the kingdom. The valley was bursting with wildflowers, all preening beneath that bright spring sun overhead. The lakes and the fields glittered with light and color, and the mountains that ringed the small country were white-capped and gleaming.

A perfect picture, she thought. *Too bad that there's nothing real beneath it.*

At the palace, she felt out of sorts and waved off the hovering staff as she took herself out into the gardens.

The palace gardens were nothing like hers had been at the manor house. They were deliberately and ruthlessly orderly. They stayed in their straight lines and even the happy colors of the spring flowers were very carefully arranged and controlled so that no *exuberance* could infect the grounds.

Walking out along the tidy paths made her feel as

if her ribs were closing in on her. As if she was being pressed to death on all sides.

Like these gardens were a prison. She felt as if she couldn't breathe.

Esme made her way down to the lake at the far edge of the gardens. It was full and deeply blue now that March was coming to an end, gleaming beneath a sun that seemed to think it was already summer. On the far side of the lake, she could see the city skyline, all those lovely old houses mixed in with newer buildings, all of them arranged along the lakefront.

It wouldn't be long now before there were boats out on the water. Landscape photographers would spend days trying to get the perfect shot to capture the lake and careful gardens with the palace above. It was part of the kingdom's allure. This fairy-tale palace. Stacked above a high mountain lake with its beautiful gardens spread out beneath an endlessly blue sky.

She didn't know why the very idea of that perfect image made her want to cry today.

"You were supposed to be in my office a half hour ago to conduct a postmortem on that wedding and any conversations that came out of it," came Tadeo's voice from behind her, jolting her out of whatever daydream had claimed her. She'd moved along the lakefront, she realized, and had wandered her way out onto one of the docks. It was clear that he must have done the same, though she hadn't heard his footfall on the wooden planks.

"As you can see, I have missed that appointment," was all she said in reply.

What she wanted to say was that she found it rich that

when women reported what they'd said and heard at a party it was considered gossip, yet when a man did it, it was *intel*. But she suspected he would find that churlish. And emotional.

She was both, but she wasn't sure she had it in her to fence words the way they usually did.

"Are you all right?" he asked again, the way he had last night, sounding… She wouldn't say *worried*. Or even *concerned*. That was all far too emotional for Tadeo, who liked all the images of his kingdom and his marriage to be aspirational and lovely and had no intention whatsoever of putting the work in on the other side.

"I'm not all right." She turned to look at him. "I'm tired of your rules, Tadeo. I know why you felt you had to set them up, but it's just one more way of distancing ourselves from what was actually going on here. What's been going on here forever."

He frowned. "The rules are the rules."

"If only you were a king, who could make any law he liked on a whim." She laughed, though there was very little mirth in the sound. "Not that that would matter, as we are not talking about the kingdom just now. We're talking about us. You and me."

"I have no desire to talk about you and me." In another mood, she might have found his tone funny. It was quite close to *panicked*, though Tadeo would never allow himself to *panic*.

Still. It was close.

"This is a love story," she told him, looking right at him. "It always has been. And you are trying to treat it like a Royal Proclamation."

"I told you almost a decade ago that love stories are not something I am built for," he growled.

But she remembered it differently. They had started telling each other that they loved each other early on. They'd said it all the time. When he'd come back from that fateful summer and had ended things with her, he'd denied he ever meant it.

The last time she'd told him she loved him she'd been sobbing, on the floor of his town house, and he'd told her he couldn't help that. That it would fade.

It had not faded.

And more importantly, he was a liar.

She had decided that he'd gaslit her at will during that hideous breakup scene. That was the story she'd told herself all throughout the next couple of years. That and he was emotionally stunted. But she'd always ended up on the fact that he was a liar.

Because she had been there.

She knew what they'd had.

She knew what he'd said.

She decided that if he was lying, he was lying to himself first.

And the past seven years proved that. The night of his father's funeral proved that. Everything that had happened since he'd learned about the pregnancy proved it.

It was never that she'd somehow gotten the wrong idea about him, or made him up in her head. She'd been right about him every step of the way.

Maybe, she thought, it was time he understood that.

"Do you know what's funny?" Esme smiled as she said that. She came close to laughing, even. "I know you *so well*, Tadeo. I know that if I say anything about love you will immediately balk, even though everything that's happened between us since you found out I was pregnant has showed me, time and again, that you're as in love with me now as ever."

He looked as if she'd struck him with an ax, but she didn't let that stop her. "That, in fact, the reason you keep coming up with all these walls to put between us is because you're still afraid of that love. But I realized recently that while I know you well enough that I can predict any response you might have and act accordingly in advance—and I do—*you* don't know *me* at all."

For a moment, he looked like she really had smashed something heavy and sharp into the side of his head.

"Of course I know you," he managed to get out after a few tense moments, when she was sure she could hear the sound of his heart. Beating too fast and too hard—or perhaps that was hers. "I don't know what this outburst is about, Esme, but it is the antithesis of our agreement."

She shook her head. "What agreement is that? I don't recall *agreeing* to anything. I went along with you. That's not the same thing."

"It is the same thing," he shot back at her. "I knew this was a mistake. I knew I shouldn't have let you into my bed again. The reality is that you can't handle it."

Esme did laugh then, directly at him. "Yes, of course. My bad. *I* am the one who can't handle it."

She could see his temper mounting. There was that thunderstorm in his blue eyes, that furious muscle in his jaw. "Do you think I don't know you?" he gritted out. "I know this. Any time there is intimacy between us, *this* is what happens. You start talking about love and it makes you impossible."

"You don't know me at all," Esme corrected him with what she hoped was a calm tone that rankled. Deeply. "For example, did you know that I don't know how to swim?"

"What?" He blinked, as if he was trying to keep up. "What does that have to do with anything? Are you quite well, Esme?"

Meaning, *Have you had a mental break?*

Because, naturally, he would think so.

"I never learned," she told him blithely. "I suppose that should have been a part of my unconventional education. What a tragedy that it was not."

Esme didn't think through what she was doing. Because she knew she was going to do it anyway, whether she thought it through or not. She turned back toward the water and then took off running down what was left of the dock, those last few feet.

Then she launched herself into the air and hit the water, plummeting down beneath the surface of the lake.

And sank.

CHAPTER NINE

FOR A MOMENT, Tadeo froze in place. In utter disbelief.

There were ripples on the surface of the lake and it was almost as if he was dreaming this, or had imagined it, or—

But in the next second, he was moving. He charged down the dock, threw himself into the air, and dived into this lake he had swum in and boated on the whole of his life. Never had he had the slightest moment of concern about these waters.

Yet everything was different now that Esme had sunk straight down and hadn't come up.

He dived deep, but there was no sign of her. And when he shot back up to the surface for a screaming sort of breath into his aching lungs, something icy and cold gripping him like a terrible fist in his chest—

But he stopped.

Because Esme was there. Floating quite happily and paddling along on the surface of the lake. He could feel his own heart like a drum. He couldn't believe what he was seeing. There was a literal red haze descending upon him, but he blinked it away.

"But you said—"

Tadeo was so furious he couldn't finish.

"I swim like a fish," Esme told him merrily. "See? You don't know me at all. As I have said."

"I thought—" But he stopped himself again, because he refused to tell her that he'd thought she was drowning. That felt like a bridge too far.

You are already in the water, fully clothed, a voice inside reminded him. *Who cares about bridges at this point?*

Still, he said nothing. If he told her she'd scared him... Well. He presumed that had been the point of this exercise and he did not wish to give her the satisfaction of telling her it had been successful.

"I want more," she told him, treading water in all her clothes. Her hair was now plastered to her head, but those luminous eyes of hers were fastened to his. "I don't want rules. I want a marriage. I want our son to grow up and know that he is loved."

"Our son will be the King of Bellaza when I am dead. He will grow up knowing this. He will understand his responsibilities—"

"He will grow up knowing that he is loved," Esme said again, with a certain steel in her voice. "Do you hear me? Better yet, do you hear yourself? Do you think that perhaps some of the challenges you faced in your childhood were due to the fact that you weren't allowed to be a child? Too concerned with responsibilities and your father's death?"

"I'm not listening to this," he growled at her. He swam to the dock and pulled himself up out of the water, then glared balefully back toward the lake. Where his queen made absolutely no move to follow him. Esme was floating on her back with her arms thrown above her head and her belly poking above the waterline, looking as if she could stay there all day. "I'm not going to take lectures on childrearing from a person so unhinged that she would throw herself into a body of water after claiming she couldn't swim for the express purpose of proving a point."

"Is that unhinged?" She lifted her feet out of the water and kicked off the singe shoe she was wearing on her right foot. Her left foot was bare. "And what point were you making, exactly, when you hauled me before you in the palace and explained to me how I must remain mute in private, like a good girl, if I wished to earn a place in your bed?"

"That was never—" But he stopped there, too.

"Do you think I don't know that you set that up so I would fail?" she asked, and though her face was tilted toward the sky, Tadeo felt that question as if she'd stabbed it into his chest like a dagger. "Of course I know." She moved in the water then, so that she was bobbing there, her solemn gaze on his. "But it didn't fail, because I'm capable of all kinds of things, Tadeo. What's a little stretch of quiet? I've been in love with you since the moment we met and you've been terrified of that, and me, and what we are together for the same length of time. To the point you lied about what you felt. And while I've managed to give you pieces of what you want along the way, you've never managed to return it, have you?"

He thought then that he had never felt colder in his life. As if he might start shattering.

"If that is true, it would seem that you've wasted a decade of your life. You should do something about that."

"Behold me doing something about it," she replied.

She swam toward him then and reached up to hold onto the dock, though she made no move to lift herself up or out. It was possible she couldn't, with her belly, but she also didn't ask him to help her.

Instead, she looked up at him and made him feel pinned to the dock where he stood.

"Have you ever asked yourself," she said quietly, those eyes of hers so intense on his, "what you would do if you could live your life on your own terms?"

"Are you mad? I am the king. I live on no terms but my own."

"Can you imagine," she said, as if he hadn't spoken, even more quietly this time, "who you would be if you hadn't let your father's fear transform you?"

Tadeo wasn't even aware of moving back, of staggering away from her as if she'd hauled off and punched him. All he knew was that she asked him that question, and he was gone. He had to put distance between them. He had to *do* something.

Anything.

He didn't know how long it took him to make it back up the hill from the lake. He was soaking wet, dressed in his dripping clothes when he came back to himself somewhere in the palace. He was also dripping on the floor.

He stood there, his head ringing and that question repeating again and again and again, until he became aware of Arturo there beside him.

"Your Majesty appears to be in need of a towel," said the older man, with his typical restraint. And understatement.

"Among other things," Tadeo muttered.

But he allowed the old servant to usher him up the back stairs through the palace, so that no one needed to see the King in his waterlogged state. A glance in the mirrors they passed suggested that his appearance would likely scare off anyone unlucky enough to venture near.

He rather alarmed himself.

His team would faint dead away.

"The Queen is in a similar state," he told Arturo when they reached his rooms. "It would be better if she did not parade through the palace as I suspect she will want to do."

"Say no more, sir," Arturo said.

"You can bring her to my office when she is dried off," Tadeo said darkly.

He showered, then dressed. And found that he was still vibrating with that same fury. Because that's what it was, he assured himself. Sheer, unadulterated fury at her temerity. At her games.

At *her*.

He walked back through the palace, taking his usual route this time. Now that he was dry and looked like himself again. Tadeo walked from his rooms, out of the private wing and down into the public areas, where courtiers bowed and curtsied as he passed and everywhere he turned his head, there were more emblems of the rich history of his country. His family.

His future.

What was important, he told himself sternly, was that a man keep a cool head so that he could better navigate the demands of his position.

As he thought that, it was like he could suddenly hear

an echo from the past. From that part of his past he much preferred to keep locked away.

He could remember walking down this same hall, headed to the same office where his father had once sat, always so clear-eyed and reserved.

Tadeo remembered how excited he'd been to share the good news about his meeting with Princess Esme with his father at last. The miraculous news, to his way of thinking—though he cringed when he thought about it now—that he had met Esme of Clarebonne, and it had gone... Better than merely *well*. Much, much better. An entire year of better.

That they were in love.

He could still remember how he'd felt that afternoon. It had been late summer outside, the lake sparkling with all the light, yet no match for how he'd felt inside. How he had been nearly bursting at the seams, so certain that his father would be delighted.

His father had impressed upon him—repeatedly—that Tadeo could make no decision more important than who he chose to marry. As a king, Tadeo would need to rely on his queen and trust her to carry out her own duties in concert with him. Royal marriages required cool heads and careful planning, King Hugo had always told him.

That was why Tadeo's marriage had been planned for him.

Never had Tadeo been so grateful for a good plan.

She is...nothing short of amazing, he had gushed when his father had waved him toward a seat and asked him what he had to say for himself. King Hugo's preferred conversation opener, even with the son he hadn't seen in many months. *She is a marvel. I do not know how it is you and her father managed to set us up so brilliantly, but I couldn't be happier. Neither one of us can believe our luck.*

He wasn't certain when it had occurred to him that his father had not responded in some time. That he only sat there, his gaze seeming cooler and more distant by the moment. Tadeo remembered when the chill in the room had finally penetrated the haze he'd been in.

How he'd felt it roll through him, like he'd suddenly found himself standing outside in a snowstorm.

Am I to understand that you have been conducting an affair with Princess Esme? King Hugo had asked. He had been sitting behind the desk, his hands folded in front of him with his usual tall, straight posture. His blue gaze had been glacial.

I suppose you could call it that, Tadeo had replied. Though he would never have called it that.

You sound besotted, his father had said in the same colorless voice.

Tadeo had laughed at that, because he hadn't been able to help himself. *I suppose I am. Isn't that wonderful?*

In retrospect, he couldn't fathom what he'd been thinking. How had he imagined that his father would have welcomed this news? But he knew the answer to that. It was Esme. It was the way Esme had talked about her parents, their warmth and kindness, their interest in their daughter that never seemed to hinge on her performance as their heir.

He had been seduced by more than simply Esme herself. He had fallen just as hard for all she represented.

No doubt he'd imagined that he would come back here and change things, simply because he'd gone and lost his head—but over the princess that had been picked out for him.

Surely that would matter.

His father's strictures about emotion couldn't apply when it was *love*. There was no possible way, Tadeo had thought.

But, *It is not wonderful, it is a disaster*, King Hugo had said, his voice frigid. *Where do you imagine this will go? Have I not told you, over and over again, that the basis of a proper and useful royal marriage is compatibility, not passion? Never passion, Tadeo.*

Yet Tadeo had known better. *Surely there is room for both.*

And he had not dared use the word that actually fit the situation.

Because even as he said it, he could see his father's face grow thunderous. *Passion becomes scandal. It is inevitable. I will have to speak to King Alain myself. There is no possible way that I can countenance this relationship. I cannot put my country in the hands of a man who allows himself to be swept away by pretty girl at a moment's notice. I thought I raised you better than this.*

Tadeo had felt as if his father had swung out and struck him. *I thought you'd be pleased. How often is it that an arranged marriage suits everyone from the start? Much less so well.*

This is not the kind of connection you should be pursuing, his father had said darkly. *What happens when the passion fades? You already know what route your mother took. Is that what you want for this country?*

Another sex scandal? More reasons to believe that the royal family is an embarrassment to the nation instead of its spine?

He had gone on like that for days. He had been relentless.

And by the time Tadeo had returned to Boston, he had been resolved to end it, because it was the least he owed the man who had given him everything. The man who had suffered so nobly for all those years in the face of so much betrayal.

How could he do anything else?

The fact that the moment he had set eyes upon Esme had been like a gut punch, that it had made him waver, only underscored what his father had said.

I don't understand, she had said then. *You said that you loved me. You know that I love you. How could there possibly be a better basis for marriage than that?*

The last thing either one of our kingdoms needs is the volatility of a love story, he had told her, parroting his father. *My people and your people deserve better.*

And he had believed that. He still believed that.

When he had summoned her to Bellaza a couple of years after their breakup, after she had graduated from college and comported herself flawlessly in London, he'd been able to see that she thought that there was a possibility that he regretted the things he'd said to her when they'd broken up.

He had made certain to make it clear that he regretted nothing.

The fact of the matter is that we're competing against a greater narrative than ourselves, he had said. It was the same thing that he'd told his father, while also making it clear that his childish infatuation with Esme had withered on the vine.

His father had believed him. He'd worked with Tadeo for years by then, and Tadeo had made sure that he never slipped like that again.

Esme had only looked at him for a long moment. *I don't know what that means*, she had said. Archly, he'd thought.

She had looked even more beautiful than he remembered, which he had considered more proof she was as dangerous to him as his father had insisted she was. He didn't want a beautiful wife. A pretty one, certainly—as he was only a man. And the people would expect no less. Even a handsome sort of woman would do, as she would be lauded for her practicality from all corners.

Tadeo had been sure that he could do better—for the kingdom, for himself—than a woman who made him feel as if his skin was being peeled off his body every time he looked at her. Who made him feel as if the world would end if he couldn't touch her. It was an outrage.

But that did not change the myth of the two of them and their betrothal, which too many people in both of their kingdoms had started to call *fate*.

How Esme had avoided hearing about this, Tadeo could not have said.

What it means is that our kingdoms have spun themselves a fairy tale, and we star in it, he had told her in as unemotional a voice as possible.

Let me guess, Esme had said. *You don't believe in fairy tales in the same way that you don't believe in love. Or happy marriages. Or anything that might make the monarchy human.*

What I believe, he had said, refusing to give in to her provocations, *is that all royal marriages are treated like fairy tales, but ours has already been written. You were betrothed to me upon your birth. Our subjects have been concocting tales about us ever since. All we have to do is ride that wave.*

Have you taken up surfing? she had asked. *How fascinating. I have never seen the appeal. Standing on objects that move very quickly on the surface of the water? No, thank you.*

He had ignored that. Especially because he had never enjoyed surfing himself, something he had not shared with her.

I would like to formally begin our courtship, he had said instead. *It will be, by necessity, extremely public. I will furnish you with a schedule. We will be seen together for a year, engaged within nine months of that year, and married at the end of that year.*

For a moment, she had only looked at him with those fathomless dark eyes of hers and he'd braced himself. He'd been certain that she would do something he hadn't thought to ward himself against. Like when he'd seen her after the breakup, very briefly, to exchange the things they'd left at each other's places and she hadn't wept. She hadn't shouted at him. She'd only looked at him, a lot like she did then, and had asked, *What do you do with the real you when you put on this mask?*

He had not answered that question.

And that day in the palace, she hadn't asked it again. Or anything like it.

She had laughed. Esme had come to the palace dressed like a Londoner. Which was to say, she had been wearing jeans tucked into boots, a chic little sweater, and minimal jewelry. She'd had her hair up in a glossy ponytail, and she had looked edible.

If he'd had any idea how long that simple meeting would end up haunting him, he was sure he would have sent a letter instead.

And why do you imagine that I would do any of those things with my ex-boyfriend? Esme had asked him. The funny part was that she had really sounded curious. As if he was a puzzle she could not figure out, which was absurd.

Even then, Tadeo had known himself to be entirely transparent in all ways. Just as his father had taught him. Just as his people deserved.

You either love your country or you don't, he had said. Perhaps a bit darkly, because exposure to her was a challenge. He'd made a mental note to up his workouts. *Which is it?*

Of course, she had murmured. *The only love you admit exists.*

Tadeo found himself thinking about all of that ancient history entirely too much as he paced about in the office now, wondering why it was taking her so long to turn up. Maybe she was still in the lake, paddling about like a happy little turtle. Maybe she had no intention of ever coming out of the water.

Either way, he knew the fault would not lie with Arturo. The old man would do his job perfectly, as he had done since before Tadeo was born.

Just as he knew that Esme would go out of her way to make it difficult, because she made everything difficult. She had been an agent of chaos from the start. He was half convinced that she was a Clarebonne spy, planted here to take down Bellaza from within.

She was halfway there.

When the door opened some while later he turned, and was unsurprised to see Esme saunter inside with her hair perfectly dried and set, meaning that she had taken her sweet time. And was challenging his own memories, for she seemed to be dressed a little too similarly to that memory he had of her in his head. The only difference was her belly, looking bigger and rounder now and reminding him that there was far more at stake here than her talk of love, or his memories of the most embarrassing year of his life so far.

Not to mention what had followed that had led them here.

Though when no one but Esme was in the room with him, it was difficult to remember why he found anything about her or the two of them embarrassing in the least.

You are your worst problem, he seethed at himself.

"If you cannot keep a civil tongue in your head about my father, I prefer you never mention him again," he told her coldly. "The man was a saint."

He didn't like the fact that instead of looking taken back at that, Esme simply looked…sad.

For him. That part was clear, and he couldn't make any sense of it.

"Is that what he told you?" she asked.

Tadeo felt his heart catapulting against his ribs again in a manner he could only call alarming. He felt the way he had down on the dock, as if the world was closing in on him. Or as if he was being sucked out and carried away to…somewhere else.

It took effort to pull himself back. Too much effort for his liking.

"This is an indisputable fact," he shot at her. "Everyone knows what he suffered. What he went through. And through it all, he stayed calm and in control of himself. What's not to admire?"

Esme moved farther into the room. He felt some kind of wave move all the way through him, rocking him. He thought that if she touched him, he might actually explode.

But she didn't come in close. She stopped a few feet from him, making him wish he'd positioned himself behind that intimidating desk.

"Have you considered the possibility that your mother wasn't the Whore of Babylon, Tadeo?" she asked. He couldn't help but notice that she seemed perfectly calm. So calm and unruffled it made him want to get his hands on her to mess her up, just a little bit. Just enough. She also wasn't done, and he did not want to hear a single word of this. "Maybe she was in love with a man who acted like an iceberg. Maybe she did what she needed to do to keep from freezing to death."

Tadeo felt everything seem to slosh about, making him feel something like drunk. Or dizzy. Maybe both. He held his hand up as if she was advancing on him when he could see that she stopped. "Don't you dare—" he thundered at her.

But Esme only nodded. "Welcome to your actual emotions, Tadeo," she said, and she didn't even sound satisfied or smug. Only that same *sad*. "This is called *feeling things*. I know you're not used to it. But you can't keep pretending they don't exist. When all along, they've been right here, just waiting for you to acknowledge them."

She turned her back on him, and there was no way she couldn't hear the way his heart was pounding so hard against his ribs. He thought they might crack into pieces. She kept going, walking across the room and sitting down in one of the chairs that helped form a little seating area by the windows.

"Why don't you tell me when you're ready to admit that you have just as many emotions as anybody else, after all," she invited him. "I know you don't want to. I know you object to being human. But Tadeo. Isn't your heart pounding?"

He'd known it. He'd *known* she could hear it.

Esme nodded, and he realized that a traitorous hand had risen up and was pressing against his chest.

But then again, she already knew.

"That's not a heart attack," she told him gently. "Those are emotions. Tadeo, I can't believe you don't remember how they feel, because I know you knew this once. I was there." She leaned forward in her chair, her gaze seeming to spear straight through him. "That's how you know you're alive."

CHAPTER TEN

Esme hoped that he couldn't tell that she was holding her breath.

She doubted that he could. He looked so *undone*. As she watched, Tadeo seemed to implode, right there before her eyes. Right there on the carpet before that massive, imposing desk that made her think of monoliths and mysterious henges, not monarchs.

If she listened hard, she was fairly sure that she could hear him *exploding*—

But he didn't. Not quite. She watched his nostrils flare. She watched him stand straighter. A moment passed. Then another. And she began to realize that she was watching him wrestle himself under control again.

He was rendering himself unto ice. Esme was watching him make himself into a sculpture that resembled him, but wasn't him. Not the real him. Not the him who *felt* and laughed, danced and loved. Not the him who had been so *alive* and so potent that the real truth was, she'd never recovered from the loss of him.

And it wasn't the first time she'd seen him do this.

"This is what you did in Boston," she said, and felt a kind of trembling deep inside—a terrible recognition. She could remember the sense of dislocation, of betrayal. How could he stand there and look like the man she'd loved and who'd loved her back so deeply and yet somehow… not be him at all any longer? How was that possible? "I watched you do it. You stood there in that living room in your Beacon Hill town house with all that wood and the sunshine pouring in and you turned yourself into an ice sculpture right in front of me."

She remembered the wood floors, old and scarred and beautiful. The sun pouring in like it was any day, even a good day, somewhere else. And all too well did she remember the stranger staring back at her from the face of the man she'd been so in love with, it actually hurt.

It still fucking *hurt*.

"You always defer to the theatrical," Tadeo told her after a moment, and he even sounded like ice now. As if all he had to do was set the temperature gauge inside himself and sooner or later, no matter what, he would freeze. "I'm not a sculpture. There's no ice involved. I am merely making certain that I'm always in control of myself."

He did not have to say, *You should take note of this skill and try it sometime*. It was implied.

"Control is feeling your emotions and choosing not to be governed by them," Esme told him, using her own control then. Not to act like a different person, but to make sure she was *herself*. "It's not pretending you don't have any emotions at all and shoving them away inside of you, so that the very hint of one is a catastrophe."

He stared at her so long she wondered if she needed to worry about frostbite. "You will forgive me if I do not intend to take advice from a woman who threw herself into a lake to make a point."

Esme shrugged. "Similarly, I am not about to be shamed by an automaton. My emotions have never interfered with the duties that I perform. But you can't say the same, can you?"

He stood straighter as if he'd been shot. As if she'd shot him through the heart when, to her recollection, it was the other way around.

"I have never failed to do my duty," Tadeo ground out, outrage in every syllable.

"To your country," Esme agreed. She leaned forward in her chair. "But what about your duties to me? I am your queen. I am your wife. I will shortly be the mother of your child. Don't you think you owe me more than all these rules and regulations you dream up purely so that you won't have to *feel* something?"

He scowled at her, but she counted reactions as victories.

"What complaints can you possibly have to make?" he demanded. He had dressed in an identical suit to the one he'd worn when he'd jumped into the lake, she noticed. His uniform. Always elegantly subdued, contained. "No one is cruel to you. I maintain you in the finest style. I am endlessly courteous to you in public, and recently, in private, we—"

It was possible, Esme thought then, that she was less in control of her emotions than she'd thought.

"First of all," she said, getting to her feet and scowling right back at him, "you seem to have forgotten who I am. It's not simply a case of you not knowing me well, it's that you seem to be laboring under the misconception that you picked me up at a roadside stand on the way to the Cape."

That muscle in his jaw flexed. "I have no such misconception."

"Do you not? Are you sure?" She drew herself up to her full height and gazed at him with all the centuries of her ancestors in her bones. "I am Princess Esme, of Clarebonne, only child and heir to my father's throne. You cannot keep me in style or at all. I keep myself." She shook her head at him. "I never *needed* you, Tadeo. I *chose* you. Even when you told me that you would court me coldly and marry me bleakly, I still chose you. I'm choosing you today as well."

And maybe she'd needed to remind herself of that, too.

"I do not understand why you insist on making all of this an amateur theatrical hour," Tadeo threw at her darkly.

But his blue eyes were wild and stormy, she could see. Filled with what she knew were feelings, though she was certain he would deny that if she pointed it out.

"I do it to wound you," she told him sweetly. "That could be my only aim, of course. I'm certain that between the two of us, with all our education and life experience, we couldn't possibly come up with another reason why a woman would choose a man."

"And how dare you suggest that I don't know who you are," he continued, and Esme wasn't sure if he was pretending she hadn't spoken or he really hadn't heard her. Another indication that he was not the ice floe he pretended he was. "I have been handed dossiers prepared about you since you were a child. I know that your favorite color is pink. That you apparently like to paint, but only on historic walls. I know that you create relationships with every single person you meet." His eyes blazed blue fire. "And you think that makes you better than other people."

"Not better," Esme corrected him, though her pulse had picked up. "Just open to other people. It's not the same thing."

"You are caring, compassionate, and kind," he told her in the same tone, but he did not sound particularly complimentary as he thundered this at her from across his office. "These are all reasons that I chose you to be my queen even after the debacle of Boston."

"Was the debacle with us that whole year?" she mused. "Or did it come back with you after you went home that summer?"

Tadeo looked like he wanted to answer that, but didn't. He pushed on. "I'm fully aware of who you are. I simply do not need nor want to immerse myself in the things that you think are necessary for a relationship. I don't even know why you insist upon it. I watched you build relationships with every staff member you've ever had. You treat them like family. What do you need with me?"

Esme blew out a breath, suddenly less interested in this fight. Because it was always a fight, and she always lost. Every time, she lost.

"I don't know how else to tell you that I love you," she said quietly. "Just as I don't know why that's meaningless to you."

Once again, he looked as if he was coming apart at the seams. As if she was piercing his flesh with knives instead of standing across from him and keeping her hands to herself.

"It's not meaningless at all," he bit out, and he sounded...*furious*, she thought. She was taken aback. He sounded something like *livid*. "I just find it psychotic."

"*Psychotic*," she repeated, stunned.

"Look at what love has wrought in this kingdom alone," he seethed at her, not quite shouting. Not quite, but close. "My mother claimed to love my father. So deeply, so desperately, that she then shared that love with every man she encountered. My father claimed he loved her too, so very much so that he enmeshed his kingdom in the dirt and grime of her exploits, tainting our family name."

"Just because they loved badly doesn't make love, itself, bad," she managed to get out, though her throat felt tight.

"What use is love?" he demanded, and he was definitely louder then. "We have something far more enduring. The legacy of both of our kingdoms and how we will usher them into the next era. Why must you always push for more than that?"

"We are *people*, Tadeo. Human beings. We are made of flesh and bone, we bleed, we cry." Even he cried, she thought, though she doubted he would admit it. "Why shouldn't we feel what everyone else feels?"

"I don't want to feel any of this," Tadeo told her starkly then, with all of that stormy fury and an undercurrent of something a lot like grief beneath it. "I tried to tell you this in Boston."

"You were lying," Esme threw at him.

But he only shook his head, and she saw there was

something grim in his gaze. "I wasn't lying. I was coming to my senses. As I'm doing now, too."

She remembered this part. That tone. That distance in his eyes.

It took everything she had not to start shaking, right there, the way she had then.

"Don't you see?" Esme realized that she was pleading with him, but she was unable to stop herself. She wasn't sure she really *wanted* to stop herself. "Your parents' relationship isn't you. It doesn't have to be *us*. We can make whatever we want out of our life. Out of this reign of ours." She blew out a breath and took a step closer to him. "You remember what it was like. I know you do. When we would lie in bed, drunk on feeling, imagining how beautiful we could make this life we got to share?"

"I do remember it," he told her, ice and fury. "And I want no part of it."

"Tadeo. You have to—"

"I don't have to do anything," he told her, and there was a terrible note of finality in his voice.

She remembered that, too.

But he was still talking. And it kept getting worse. "It was a terrible idea to bring you into the palace. I will be removing you immediately. You can go back to the manor house, and you will stay there. You will only emerge to perform your official duties."

"Are you putting me in jail, Tadeo?" she asked him, though her throat felt tight. "Again?"

If he heard her, he gave no sign. "When the child is born, he will stay there and make it his primary residence until he's old enough to have his own room in the palace. We will never divorce. You can wander the palace grounds, flinging yourself into lakes and violating the walls of the historic buildings you encounter to your heart's content. You can scream into the wind. You can dance in the rain. I don't care. But Esme." And his blue eyes seemed to tear into her. "You will not do it with me."

"Tadeo," Esme whispered, her heart pounding, something like a headache starting at her temples.

But he was already moving. Across the room and to the door, flinging it open to bark orders down the hall.

And he was the king. What he said happened, immediately.

It was Arturo who collected Esme, apologizing profusely and politely while he herded her back out the family entrance she'd used the day she'd come here to live, and into a waiting car.

"Her Majesty's belongings will follow later today," he assured her.

Esme paused, half in and half out of the car, and caught the loyal old retainer's gaze.

"I hope you take care of him," she said quietly. Intently. "Because you know no one else will."

Arturo inclined his head. "Madam," he said in the same tone, "that is my raison d'etre. You may depend upon it."

Then he closed the car door behind her and tapped on the roof to let the driver know she was ready.

Esme wanted to cry out—scream, maybe—that she was anything but ready. Instead, she let herself sit back. She stared out the window, though she saw nothing but that look on Tadeo's face.

The drive back to the manor house was painful.

But not as painful as when they dropped her off in the drive in front of the house, and she found herself staring at the facade of the building. First because she didn't see it. Then because she did.

"What did you expect?" she asked herself fiercely, her voice a rough scrape that the breeze stole away.

She didn't know what she expected. That it would be left as a monument? That they would simply leave her paints be?

It shouldn't feel like a slap that they hadn't. That the manor house now looked precisely the way she'd first seen it. Elegant, austere.

A jail. The same jail she'd been sent to on her wedding night. This was like being caught in a time loop. Would it be another seven years before he touched her again?

Could she bear it?

She walked inside, and saw that they had redone the interior, too. It even smelled like fresh paint.

Everything was muted again. All her bright colors were gone, covered up, erased. She felt her pulse begin to get rapid, a lot like she was having a panic attack, and so she forced herself to take deep breaths as she walked down the long, main hall toward the back of the house. So she could see what they'd done to the gardens.

That wasn't a surprise either. But she found herself sobbing all the same, because they'd cut down all her flowers. They'd mulched up her wildflower beds. They hadn't let spring do with this private, unseen, unvisited garden what it would.

Because it didn't send the right *message*.

Esme stood on the terrace and she let the tears come.

She held her belly tight, and as she bowed her head, she cried.

It was as if she could see it all spool out, how the years would pass.

He would keep her here. Over time, she would stop... being herself, because there would be no point. He would take her child and call it *duty. Responsibility.* He was very unlikely to have another one with her, even though it was something they had promised each other when they'd signed their wedding documents. Not because a winter masquerading as a man really wanted children, but because of the dynastic implications and thrones in play.

But either way, if they did have a second child, she imagined he would take that child, too, and teach them to be little versions of him. Snow and ice and nothing nice, that was what her children would be made of, and the very idea made her feel sick.

She would be left here. To paint the walls or perhaps creep around them, peeling off the wallpaper, like the book she'd read again and again in college.

A book about a woman driven mad by a world—and a husband—that wanted her to conform, not *live*.

And all the while Esme would know that if she'd just done as he'd asked and had never gone looking for him after his father's funeral, she would have been free of all this by now.

But even as she thought that, everything in her revolted at the idea. She cried a bit more, and then wiped at her eyes, because she couldn't quite countenance this level of self-pity. Despite what Tadeo thought, there was a fine line between feeling her own feelings and theatrical productions of them.

She wiped at her face again, then smoothed her hands over her belly.

"I would rather have you than be done with all this," she told her baby, fiercely. "I would pick you, over and over again."

She felt a quick series of kicks at that and it made her smile right there on that empty terrace, with her destroyed garden in front of her.

And she knew, with a deep down, bedrock certainty, that she was going to be okay.

That no matter what happened and no matter what Tadeo thought he was going to do, Esme was going to be just fine. She would make certain that her baby was too.

This meant that she had no intention whatsoever of allowing Tadeo to raise their child to follow in his chilly footsteps. Duty and responsibility were all very well, and even necessary given the family business, but they weren't everything.

Her child was not going to grow up frozen solid from the inside out.

She took a deep breath and blew it out again. Then she turned and walked back into the manor house, now fully restored to its historic glory, and pale because of it.

Esme had no intention of becoming a series of elegant, empty rooms that were pretty enough to walk through yet left nothing of themselves behind.

She would not stop fighting. She would not succumb to despair.

Not this time.

He could only toss her aside if she let him. Because

despite everything, she still knew the truth. She still knew not only who she was, but who *he* was, too. She had always known. She hadn't fallen in love with herself in Boston. She hadn't made up what happened between them.

There was no possibility that she could have loved him this long if he was truly as inaccessible as he wished he was.

The only way for love to fail, she thought, was for it to be given up on.

Until then, it was simply a matter of time.

Esme had a lifetime.

And she intended to start using it.

CHAPTER ELEVEN

THE MATTER OF Esme was finally settled, Tadeo thought. There had been too many years of turmoil, but that was finished now. He had outlined the future for her, he had accepted that no other future was possible, and that was that.

He expected to settle down into the day's work without sparing so much as a thought for errant wives or replaying unpleasant conversations. After all, there were ministers to meet with, dignitaries to soothe and flatter, and the business of the kingdom to occupy him.

Tadeo was sure that the stranglehold Esme had held him with for all this time was gone, now. He was certain that she would simply be another obligation he thought about only when necessary, and—once she was no longer necessary—not at all.

Starting today, he thought with satisfaction, *I am a new man.*

But that was not quite how it went.

He couldn't seem to sit still at his own desk. His mind kept wandering. He kept running over and over all the things that Esme had said to him, and it was as if she was saying them to him all over again. He was having the same reaction. He could hardly catch a damned breath.

After a while, he realized he was wearing a groove into the rugs in his office, he was pacing so much. He sat in meetings and could not have been asked to repeat what was said to him. He could not concentrate on *messaging* or social media campaigns or the various reactions of the press to the news of Esme's pregnancy when all he could think of was Esme herself.

We can make whatever we want out of our life, she had said, as if that was easy. Or possible. Or permitted. *Out of this reign of ours.*

As if it had always been theirs, to do with as they pleased. It was laughable.

But he was not laughing. *You remember what it was like*, she had said. *I know you do. When we would lie in bed, drunk on feeling, imagining how beautiful we could make this life we got to share?*

He did remember. He remembered too well. That feeling of possibility, of limitless horizons. That scandalous, glorious feeling that the two of them truly could beat all the odds—because they already had. They'd expected to find each other passable at best. Nice enough, even.

Instead, one look and they'd *ignited*.

It had to mean that they could change their whole worlds—Tadeo remembered how deeply and fully he'd believed that. With Esme at his side, there was nothing he couldn't accomplish.

But his father had set him straight. He'd always been so grateful for that. He'd spent all the years he'd had left with his father making up for that lapse. He'd gone out of his way to prove to King Hugo that he had a worthy successor.

And Esme had made him question all of that. *Have you considered the possibility that your mother wasn't the Whore of Babylon?* she had asked.

When Tadeo knew exactly who his mother was. Exactly who everyone knew his mother was. That hadn't changed simply because Esme wanted to be difficult.

Still, he couldn't seem to get her words out of his head. *Maybe she was in love with a man who acted like an iceberg*, Esme had said, and it had punched straight through him. *Maybe she did what she needed to do to keep from freezing to death.*

It occurred to Tadeo then that he'd never considered his father cold, only correct.

But if he wasn't...

Later, he found himself pacing through the palace, and he must have had a fierce enough expression on his face because no one attempted to speak to him. In fact, they stepped out of his way, bowed their heads, and kept their eyes averted.

A lot like he was having the sort of emotional episode he wanted—badly—not to be capable of.

Tadeo found himself in the portrait gallery yet again, looking at the faces of his ancestors as if they could offer him some clues. Looking at his own wedding portrait that he'd always thought had adequately captured what their marriage was. Cordial, but appropriately separate. Cold, certainly, but that had been representative of the relationship they'd had then. The relationship he'd assumed they'd always have.

He'd already realized, since Esme's pregnancy had

been revealed, that he'd been ignoring how sad she looked in the portrait. Somehow he'd always believed that she simply looked like a queen. Appropriately solemn—but no.

She looked like she wanted to cry.

Tonight he was horrified to discover that even looking at the painting now made him...

Something in him balked. He didn't want to name it. He didn't want to call this what it was, because that gave it a power—

Sad, something in him whispered, sounding a great deal like Esme herself. *That's the word you're looking for. Sad.*

The last time he could remember using that word to describe his state, he'd been eleven years old. His mother had died under less-than-ideal circumstances—gallivanting about, quite publicly, with a lover on a boat near Crete—but his father had decided to give her the state funeral her position demanded.

A funeral fit for the queen, nay, the woman *she should have been*, the self-righteous television anchor had intoned.

It had been a somber affair. Now, looking back, Tadeo found himself wondering if everyone had been aware that it was all for show on his father's part. Some believed he was simply *that good*, certainly. But surely there had to be others who wondered if, perhaps, King Hugo had been going to a great deal of trouble to prove that he had been the decent spouse. That he was self-sacrificing even to the end, and even in the face of his wife's outrageous behavior.

Someone had to have wondered if, perhaps, he'd been

protesting too much. If they did, they did it quietly. The papers had already been calling King Hugo a saint.

But eleven-year-old Tadeo hadn't known anything about *messaging*, or the manipulation of the press.

What he'd known was that his mother was dead. Moreover, that he was highly discouraged from commenting on that or displaying any of the many emotions he felt about that death in public.

Why are you making that face? his father had asked as they had walked soberly and slowly behind Marisol's coffin through the streets of the kingdom. *You are being watched, Tadeo. A certain decorum is expected from a future king and it is best you exhibit it.*

I'm sad, Tadeo had said to his father. Not the King, just…his father. *I'm just sad.*

But Hugo had not spared him a glance. He had continued his slow and precise pace, his back straight and tall, his eyes forever forward. *Don't be so maudlin*, he'd said, in that cold, dismissive way of his that had settled deep into Tadeo's bones. *You are the Crown Prince of Bellaza. You are, by definition, never anything so pedestrian as* sad.

Over the years, Tadeo had decided that his father had been trying to give him a pep talk. That Hugo had been trying to keep Tadeo's spirits up while they saw to such a grim task, and more, while they did so under such intense scrutiny.

It had been a great kindness, Tadeo had decided. He would have argued about it, had anyone dared ask. *Not all kindnesses feel good*, he would have said. *There is no law that insists it* must *feel warm and fuzzy, only that it do what it is meant to do.*

But now…

He thought of his child, his son, still nestled deep inside Esme's belly. He thought of the nights he'd spent smoothing his own hands over her belly, murmuring to the child within.

Tadeo had not met his son yet and yet try as he might, he could not imagine telling that child that he could not be sad at a funeral. His own mother's funeral, no less. Even if he and Esme remained as much at odds as they were now forever, he would not expect *her child* to react stoically to her passing.

Even if Esme behaved in ways Tadeo did not like, how could that possibly dictate the behavior of her own child in the face of her death?

These thoughts tore at him. He felt a kind of fissure open up inside him, yawning wide, and he had the strangest feeling that there would be no closing it again. That there would be no repairing this.

He just didn't know what that meant.

When he heard footsteps, he schooled his expression to the expected neutrality—but was pleased when he saw that it was Arturo. Possibly even relieved.

"It grows late," the most loyal of all the servants in the palace said, and whatever expression Tadeo had on his face, Arturo would never appear to notice it. "Would His Majesty care for dinner in his rooms, perhaps?"

Tadeo didn't move. He couldn't seem to look away from the portrait of his parents now. It was like it was calling to him. "You remember my parents better than I do. You were here when my father was growing up."

Arturo did not change his own expression by so much as the faintest twitch. "It has been my great honor to serve three generations of the Santiago family, Your Majesty."

"All I know are stories." Tadeo ran his hands over his face. "Stories in the papers, stories from my father." He looked at the old man. "What do you remember? What really happened?"

He didn't know, until he said the words out loud, how much seemed to ride on the answer.

For a long moment, he thought the other man wouldn't reply. Arturo had been in the palace for so long that he was, in many ways, the finest example of royal protocol there was. It was possible he would think that he had no business discussing such matters and therefore would not. It would not matter if the King himself commanded him to do so.

But after a moment he cleared his throat, and when Tadeo looked at him again, he had a curious look on his face.

That fissure inside Tadeo…widened.

"Your father was a strange boy," Arturo said after a moment, which was perhaps the last thing Tadeo would have expected anyone to say about King Hugo. "Oddly still. Decent to all, if robotic. But one does not speculate about such things, not if one wishes to remain in the palace. I watched him grow up and he was always the same."

"He valued constancy," Tadeo said, agreeing.

He realized he was frowning and forced himself to stop.

The older man looked at him, a canny sort of light in his gaze. "Did he value it, or was it all he was capable of?" he asked, in his quiet way.

And something inside Tadeo went terribly still.

He had a sudden flash of memory then. It was something he had overheard his mother say when he was very young.

Tadeo had been playing in a part of the palace where he'd been told many times not to go. He'd heard his mother with her voice raised, which usually meant she was talking to his father. *Just because you can't feel anything doesn't mean you should dictate to the rest of us who have the full spectrum of human emotion*, she had thrown at the King.

In return, he had heard his father's slow, measured tones, but not the words he'd used.

His mother had responded with a wild laugh. *I would never wish to be like you*, she had said. *I would rather die.*

Tadeo had known better than to get caught listening to his elders without their knowledge. He'd ducked back down one of the servants' stairs and had hurried away.

Now, here in the portrait room, Arturo shifted from one foot to the other. "I cannot excuse what your mother did extramaritally," he said, and sounded as if he was being very careful. Almost *judicious*. "But I will tell you that it was done deliberately. To prove a point."

"I don't know what that means," Tadeo managed to get out, though his jaw felt like granite.

"My understanding is that her first affairs were in private," Arturo continued in that same, measured tone. "And the King, may he rest in peace, did not care at all. He only cared when her affairs were public. Because what he cared about was not the infidelity, if you catch my meaning. It was that other people knew of it."

Tadeo felt himself getting...overly warm. As if he was sweating. As if he was *flustered*.

As if a pedestal was crashing to the ground and taking him with it.

It was as if Arturo knew it. As if he could see it too. "What I am trying to tell you, Your Majesty, is that I am not certain that King Hugo—for all his many virtues and may he rest in peace—was *capable* of caring about anything besides the kingdom. Or if he was, I never saw it."

The full import of those words took a moment to settle on Tadeo. When they did, they landed hard. He felt as if the old man had taken a swing at him. And had landed a knockout punch.

"Including me, is what you mean," he said when he was able to speak.

Though his voice sounded unlike his. Too rough. Too raw.

Arturo looked him straight in the eye, which was revolutionary and upsetting itself. "It is my observation that your father went to great lengths to teach you how to tamp down the emotions that he never felt himself, Your Majesty. Not because he truly felt that they would impact on your ability to be a good king, but because he didn't like them."

Tadeo knew, then, what he would say. He knew, and yet he could do nothing to stop what was coming. He could not repair that widening chasm inside him. He could not *breathe*.

"They reminded him too much of your mother," Arturo said, inevitably, and Tadeo let that settle on him too, like so much granite and despair. "King Hugo preferred things tidy and always precisely the same. Do you see what I mean, sir? He never thought of himself as empty. So he emptied out those around him instead, so that they would match."

And Tadeo had no idea how long he stood there, staring in something that wasn't quite as simple as shock at the portrait of his father on the wall.

Yet all he could see was Esme.

All he could *hear* was Esme. All the things she'd said to him over the years, and today. All the accusations she'd laid at his feet that he'd swept away, so certain that *she* was the problem.

Because a man who couldn't feel at all had told him that he felt too much.

And then it was as if Esme was a great swell inside him, growing like a wave, taking him over, knocking him down—

But Tadeo did not fall.

Instead, he ran. He ran through the halls of his own palace, leaving stunned and shocked courtiers in his wake—and for once he did not care at all. He could not have been less interested in what *message* he was sending.

Tadeo ran until he found one of his vehicles parked out by one of the garages, ignored his guards, and jumped behind the wheel.

He set off for the manor house, driving the roads of the royal estate far too quickly. Time seemed to press in on him, and inside himself, he felt certain that it was running out.

That it might very well be too late already.

The night was dark but clear, and the stars were so bright they felt very nearly blinding. He felt almost as if he was drunk, though he knew full well he was not. The road wound down the hillside, cutting through the fields on the back side of the palace, and Tadeo took one turn so fast that when he saw the headlights coming in the opposite direction on the single-lane road he had no choice but to drive off to the side, narrowly missing a stout, medieval hedge.

The oncoming car stopped. He heard the window roll down.

"Are you all right?" came Esme's clear, concerned voice through the dark.

Tadeo felt that wave wash over him all over again. That chasm in him seemed to stop growing. Time released its pressure.

She didn't even know it was him, he thought. It could have been anyone. And yet she, the Queen, stopped her vehicle and inquired after his safety when she was the one who was six months pregnant.

The fissure had stopped growing, he realized then, because it had torn down all the armor he'd worn, all the walls he'd built, all the things he'd built his life around because he'd thought that was the *proper* way to do it.

Everything she had said to him was true. Her emotions didn't inhibit her or diminish her. They only made her stronger. They made her better. They made her...*her*.

The bright light that was *her*—far brighter than her headlights that picked up the wide expanse of royal acreage on either side of them.

Tadeo pushed his way out of the car. Esme was getting out of hers, more awkwardly these days with her pregnant belly. She stopped when she saw him, her jaw dropping open a bit.

"Tadeo?" Her voice was little more than a whisper, as if she didn't believe her own eyes.

But finally he thought that he believed his.

There were stars above, and Esme was here, and for the first time in so long—ten whole years—everything made sense.

He hadn't realized how empty he'd felt until now, when he finally felt whole.

When he finally understood the whole story of not just his life, but his father's and his mother's and all the ways they'd led him here.

"I was coming to look for you," Esme said after a moment, sounding...thrown, perhaps. But she rallied. He saw her square her shoulders. "I have something to say to you, Tadeo."

"Say it," he bade her, and he leaned back against the boot of his car and folded his arms, because if she wanted to talk to him, he would listen.

This time he would listen as if his life depended on it and he would keep his father out of his head while he did.

"The manor house has been desecrated," she told him, very seriously. "It smells like new paint and regret. It's pale and sad and diminished." She moved closer to him and then she pointed her finger directly at his chest. "That's what you want to do to me, Tadeo. And I won't allow it."

She wasn't wrong, and he would have to live with that. But that was for later.

Now, he shook his head. "I doubt you could ever be diminished, Esme."

He did not expect her to scowl at him, much less so ferociously. "Don't patronize me, please. I have no intention of letting you shuffle me off again. I don't know why I put up with it for seven years. I kept thinking that if I was perfect enough, if I was dutiful enough, I would somehow live up to whatever paragon it is you have in your head. I thought that I could prove that even though we were blessed with the chemistry that drew us together, I was also capable of being the perfect queen for you. I think I did that, Tadeo. I think I pulled it off." She pulled in a deep breath. "It still wasn't enough for you."

He said nothing, but she moved closer still. He watched her as her gaze searched his, and could not begin to imagine what expression he wore.

She frowned, so he assumed it was unusual. "On the night of your father's funeral, I only wanted to comfort you. But it turned into something else and I realized the truth. *That* was the real reason you never wanted to be alone with me. Because there was no getting away from it, is there? There's never been any escaping who we are to each other." Another breath, like she was preparing herself. Her chin rose. "And I'm not going to facilitate it anymore."

She was even closer now and Tadeo felt nothing inside him but that great wave and swell that was all her, always her. It was beautiful Esme, the mother of his child. Esme, his queen. Esme, who had knocked his world off its axis by smiling at him outside a Boston restaurant on that fateful first evening.

Esme, the woman who had loved him when he most certainly did not deserve it for the past ten years.

He reached over and pulled a thick lock of her dark hair between his fingers, then rolled it back and forth.

Her breath stuttered slightly. He saw a flash of heat

along her cheekbones. "What are you doing?" She frowned, but it looked to him as if summoning it took work. "Why aren't you putting up your usual fight?"

And then, at last, it was Tadeo's turn.

He was determined to get this right.

"Esme," he said, tasting her name on his mouth the way he'd used to do, as if it was some kind of sweet liquor that could only go to his head. "I have been fighting against you since the day we met. You came in like a storm, swept me away, and I never found my footing again."

"You didn't need your footing. You have a crown."

He tugged slightly on the lock of her hair, and she subsided. "I tried my best. I broke up with you in a way calculated to hurt you the most. I insisted on a cold pageant of a wedding, and worse still, a frigid marriage. And you went along with all of those things. You went along with them, and I intended to reward you for that service by divorcing you."

"Yes," Esme agreed, though she looked...not quite *confused*. Something more like *wary*. "You're the worst man I know. I have no idea what I see in you."

"Nor do I," he assured her. "But tonight, if you will allow it, I want to make you a new kind of vow."

He moved in closer then and he took her hands in his, and was cheered when she gripped him in return.

"I was told that love is a fantasy, and emotions are weakness. That my country required me to lock those things away and hide them where they could never be seen, never be felt, and never, ever shown to those around me." He lifted her hands to his mouth and pressed a kiss on her knuckles. "And what has that made me? An ice sculpture, as you say."

Esme's eyes were wide, now. He could see the pulse in her throat going wild.

"Everything I know is inside out," he told her, his voice low and raw, because perhaps that was what truth did when it finally came out. It left marks. "It is possible my father was simply incapable of feeling anything and considered that his greatest virtue. Perhaps he decided that those who did not possess that virtue the way he did—meaning everyone around him—were disappointments. Maybe my mother simply refused to keep the parts of herself locked away as he demanded."

It was his turn to blow out a breath, and he did, then held her hands tighter. "When I came home from Boston that summer and told my father that I'd fallen in love with the woman that everyone expected me to marry—an absolute miracle of epic proportions—he was horrified. I should have realized that was his problem, not mine. But I had been raised on a steady diet of my mother's scandalous behavior and my father's noble attempts to keep his head up high despite them, and I believed he knew better."

He held her gaze intently, then. "I'm sorry for that. I'm sorry for not defending something so beautiful from the start."

He felt the jolt that went through her, and saw the emotion in her eyes.

But he wasn't finished. "You were the only one I wanted anywhere near me at my father's funeral, but I could never admit that to myself. I was relieved when you found me. And I remember exactly who started that kiss that night. It was me. Filled with all those emotions I would have told you I didn't know how to feel and just drunk enough to hope no one would notice."

"Tadeo, I don't know—" she began.

"I cannot bear the thought of raising our child like that," Tadeo continued, urgently. "I can't imagine turning my son against his mother. I can't imagine pretending that you're not the reason I even know what love is." He let out a rusty sort of laugh. "I fought so hard against it, Esme. I gave that fight my all. And yet every time, no matter how hard I fight, I come straight back to you."

He found he was holding his breath then.

Esme gazed up at him, her hands in his and her eyes wide and solemn, and once again he wondered if he was too late. If he'd taken too long. If he'd lost her, after all.

Then he saw her smile, and it was as if she took all the stars from the sky and aimed them straight at him.

"You do," she said softly. "And I want you to do that. I don't think you ever had a safe space in your life, for all you have palaces and manor houses and servants, and royal compartments that could house a crowd."

"The only fight I'm interested in," Tadeo told her, intensely, "is fighting for you, my Esme. Even if the enemy I must fight is me."

"I have an idea." She moved closer to him and she pressed that heavy stomach of hers against him and looped her arms around his neck as best she could. She gazed up at him, and he felt like they made a perfect circle, there beneath the stars at last. The two of them, their foreheads touching. The baby they'd made pressed in between their bodies. "Why don't we start over?"

"Can we do such a thing?" he asked, but he realized he was smiling.

In private, not for a camera or a political reason.

A real smile, for the first time since Boston.

"You will have to ask the king of this realm," Esme told him, her smile wider. She ran her fingers through his hair. "He is *very* powerful. He can do whatever he likes."

"It sounds like you have an in with him." Tadeo let that smile of his do what it liked. And her too. "I like your chances."

She smiled up at him and then her smile faded as she traced her fingers over his face, as if she was learning his contours all over again.

"So do I," she whispered. "So do I, my love."

He captured her hand and held it to his cheek.

"I love you," he told her, with all the solemnity and intensity of a vow made in cathedrals in the presence of most of Europe. Though it was better now. It was only them. "You were right. I have loved you since the moment we met, and I have loved you badly. All I can hope for is that you will let me spend the rest of our lives making it up to you."

"I don't need you to make anything up to me," Esme told him, and there were tears on her face, but joy in her gaze. "All I need from you is *you,* Tadeo. Because between us, we can do anything, whether it's change the way we rule these kingdoms or love each other the way we deserve."

"I want that," he whispered. "Though I doubt I deserve—"

She put her hands on his mouth and stopped him. "We have wasted too much time to dwell in the past. We have a baby coming, and I want him to know us like this. In love. In harmony." He kissed the fingers on his mouth and she smiled. "We can do it. I *want* to do it, Tadeo. With you or not at all."

And from that day forward, because he was indeed the king of all he surveyed and particularly of this sheltered valley in a remote section of the Pyrenees, Xavier Tadeo Santiago, King of Bellaza, made it so.

CHAPTER TWELVE

Like everything else he had ever done, which was no surprise to Esme, Tadeo took to love as if it was something upon which he would be tested. And might fail at any point.

They did not sleep apart. Ever. He told her that he loved her as often as possible.

"Someday," she said with a laugh, "you might even say that without sounding as if you're worried that the words might bite you back."

He was lying next to her in their bed that time. And he looked at her, his expression a mix of affront and astonishment.

"Loving is perilous," he said. "For my heart. You will have to excuse me if it takes some getting used to."

But he got used to it.

Because of course he did. The first thing he did was get rid of that monolithic desk from the king's office. He did not explain why, though Esme had her suspicions. It was consigned to some far-off corner of the palace, never to cross the King's eyesight again.

And in its place, Tadeo installed a lovely, wooden desk that caught the sun and gleamed in a way that reminded both of them of that marvelous old town house of his in Beacon Hill.

Before the baby was born, he took Esme back to Clarebonne, so that her people could cheer for her—or that was what he said. But Esme rather thought it was to show her parents that things were better between them now. Thawed.

"Do my eyes still look sad?" Esme asked her mother on one of their walks.

Luisa had her arm laced through her daughter's, and she squeezed it tight. "Not a drop," she said.

Their son was born two weeks late, a squalling, dark-haired slice of perfection, who they both fell in love with immediately. They called him Alain for Esme's father, a man to admire and look up to. And Hugo, for Tadeo's father, as a chance to shine brighter.

But the name they used was Enrique, and Enrique was a delight.

One night after she nursed him, Tadeo held the baby and soothed him to sleep in his arms, looking something like stricken when Esme caught his gaze.

"I had no idea," he said, hoarse.

"About what?" Esme asked.

"That it was supposed to feel like this all along," he whispered. "So huge. Almost painful. But so beautiful, Esme. Incapacitatingly beautiful."

"That is exactly how it's supposed to feel," she told him, coming over to the chair where he sat and kissing him on his temple.

He reached up and smoothed his palm over her cheek. "When I met you, I felt like this and I thought something was wrong. I thought it had to be a mistake. Something to fight and get over." His eyes glistened, and Esme's heart thumped. "I'm so glad you never let me."

Esme leaned down and kissed him on his mouth. "And I never will," she promised him.

She gave birth to their daughter three years later and called her Marisol Luisa, though the family knew her as Soli. She was made of grit and sunshine, and even the older brother she tortured was besotted with her.

Together, the two of them would rule the two kingdoms.

Esme considered it her job to make sure that they never lost themselves in the jobs that waited for them. And when it came to the future Queen Soli of Clarebonne, Esme and her daughter spent as much time as possible with the expert on that topic. Luisa.

On one such visit, when Luisa had come to Bellaza and was walking in the gardens with her granddaughter, engrossed in very serious conversations with the small girl, Esme stood by a window and watched them.

Her parents were not simply grandparents to her children, Enrique and Soli and the three others she'd had after them because she and Tadeo could not seem to think of a good reason *not* to have the big family they'd always wanted as only children. Over the years, she had watched her parents stand in, in many ways, for the parents Tadeo had never had.

They had showed him the love he had always deserved.

And she had watched her husband bloom into the man she'd always known he could be. The man she'd fallen in love with so long ago.

"I pinch myself every day that we get to live like this,"

he told her one night as they danced at some glimmering ball, surrounded on all sides by the toast of Europe—though Esme had eyes only for Tadeo. "Like everything is magic, no matter what challenges come our way."

She tilted back her head and smiled at him. "I love you too," she said. "And the best part is, the magic only gets better as we go along."

Esme knew that this was true. Because she knew that all the way on the other end of the palace estate there stood a manor house. And maybe one day, when she was gone, her daughters would congregate there and wrinkle up their noses, and restore the place to some former ideal of sophistication and elegance.

Assuming she had failed to raise them right, that was.

But in these years, when they needed a night away from the palace and their boisterous family, Esme and Tadeo would liberate one of the royal vehicles and take off across the back roads in the dark, and they would paint like wild animals and laugh all the while.

They would make love to each other in every single one of the rooms, moving into intensity and joy and holding space for the sorrows of life brought, and the inevitable scars they carried.

But all of that became beautiful, because it was shared.

Because it was allowed to be bright and messy, a visual cacophony of the secrets their hearts carried.

When her children grew older and asked Esme to tell the story of how their parents had met, she told him the truth. With only a few details omitted, to protect their tender sensibilities. She showed them that terrible portrait in the gallery and pointed out how stiff and sad both she and their father looked.

"Because we were," she would say.

And as they gasped and laughed and were scandalized by their father's seemingly tyrannical behavior, Tadeo would laugh too. He would hold Esme on his lap and smile at all the fine young humans they were raising to feel every single thing they felt—but learn how to control it, too.

"Lucky for me," he would always tell them, "your mother loves me well enough that I learned to love myself, and her, and all of you, too."

He also commissioned a new portrait for their fiftieth anniversary, a far better representation of the two of them. The same pose. The same people. But the love they shared poured out of the canvas and lit up the whole of that gallery.

And if this was the happy-ever-after that she got, Esme liked to think, it was worth those ten years of uncertainty. It was worth everything. Given the chance, she would do it again.

In a heartbeat.

That was the kind of thing she told only Tadeo, tangled around him in the bed they shared, where he could respond to her in the only way that mattered. The only way that made both of their hearts beat out the same rhythm.

Because it was perfectly clear to the both of them that they had always been meant to be one, all along.

And now they always would be.

* * * * *

If you loved King's Heir of Hate, *make sure to read*

Sicilian Devil's Prisoner.

This fantastically dramatic romance by Caitlin Crews is available now!

CHAPTER ONE

Birds sang in the thick green trees as they danced through the dense, overgrown gardens outside the magnificent old villa some thirty minutes from the center of Palermo, Sicily. But what Giovanbattista D'Amato—called Jovi by the few who dared address him directly—noticed despite their chatter were the sounds that should not have been there, soft beneath the usual noises he knew so well.

It seemed he had a guest.

When he was not the kind of man who encouraged visitors, especially of the uninvited persuasion. Something that must surely be clear by the untended sprawl of gnarled oleander and fig trees that had grown up around the gates down near the road and made the entrance to the villa seem all the more secretive and, therefore, more provocative.

The villa was perfectly preserved and stunning, as everyone always whispered in shocked tones, *despite everything*. Teenagers and tourists who thought they might poke around a place with such a riveting, tragic past were usually scared off by their own overactive imaginations long before they made it to the villa's front door.

The ghosts that haunted the villa and its quiet slide toward a graceful, genteel ruin knew only too well how to occupy a mind and sneak deep into an unguarded moment.

Jovi knew that better than anyone.

He heard the car out in the front of the villa, on the winding drive that had given way to the demands of changing seasons and the scrubby mountainside that stretched above and below, though nothing could conceal the bones of the estate, a crowning achievement of the Sicilian Baroque period. Neither time nor negligence could dim its glamour in the slightest.

Jovi had certainly tried.

He heard the slam of the car's heavy door, yet he stayed where he was. He sat perfectly still in the shade of the towering oak tree some gardener long-dead had planted here in another lifetime, as if he was contemplating nothing more than the easy mysteries of a warm, Sicilian afternoon.

But that was only the impression others might form if they saw him here, sitting so quietly.

And only those who didn't know him.

Because anyone who knew Giovanbattista D'Amato knew exactly who and what he was. Ice, straight through.

Ice where other men were flesh. Ice in place of organ and bone.

He remained still. He supposed that it was possible that somewhere, back in the dimness of the youth he did not allow himself to recall too closely—or too often, lest he give those ghosts free rein—he had gone ahead and taught himself these skills he used without thought, now.

The ability to sit so still that the birds themselves mistook him for a statue. A stone like any other.

The capacity to wait. To do nothing else. To simply *wait*, without moving. Without breathing too much, lest it make his chest move and differentiate him from the stone walls. To easily parse the various sounds that reached his ears. The birds. The breeze and the trees above. The rustle of small creatures in his gardens, long since surrendered to riots of rogue blossoms and weeds—a rebellion against the meticulously maintained, award-winning planting concepts that had once been synonymous with the villa and its residents.

He identified all of those, set them aside, and listened for the heavy fall of a man's leather shoe inside the graceful, empty rooms of the once-proud villa that rose up behind him.

Jovi did not lock the place. Why should he? Terrible things had already happened here and there was no pretending otherwise. There was nothing to steal that he could not replace, assuming that he could be bothered. To his way of thinking, anyone was welcome to drop in. Unannounced and heavily armed, if they wished.

Though they might wish otherwise. Quickly.

He was not concerned about people entering this place where he lived when he was in Sicily. Because he knew that the difficulty was not in the entering. But in the leaving.

Once someone invaded his space, they would leave it again only if *he* wished it.

His were the only wishes that he would allow to prevail on this sprawling parcel of land, set up on the rugged mountainside, claimed by men who must have imagined it was ever truly possible to escape the chokehold of Sicily.

Jovi knew better.

He heard feet on one side of the duel staircases in their Sicilian Baroque style, all high drama as they marched away from each other and then angled back to meet at the great door.

And as the footsteps drew closer, he heard the faintest sound. Like a rough laugh, checked before it was anything more than a breath.

No need, then, to worry about his response.

He waited instead. And when the footsteps drew even closer, barely making scraping sounds across overgrown flagstones crafted by the finest stonemakers in Sicily and left to the whims of the sun, there was another laugh. This one untethered, likely because its owner thought he was alerting Jovi to his presence.

The way he always did.

"I don't know how you live in this haunted place," came the intruder's familiar, disparaging voice.

Not an intruder, Jovi corrected himself. Not exactly.

He did not bother to turn around. He knew who his uninvited guest was. Had known, in truth, the moment he'd heard that particular heavy cadence of footfalls from inside the villa.

Carlo D'Amato, his cousin. His oldest cousin and his uncle's favorite son. This meant Carlo was also considered the *sotto capo* of what some news organizations liked to call the *D'Amato crime family*, but only because they dared be disrespectful from the distance afforded them through newsprint.

To those who knew better than to show disrespect,

they were known as Il Serpente, wily enough to outwit the many criminal investigations that had plagued families like theirs since back in the 1800s. Not to mention the rival criminal organizations who muscled in where they could.

Most shivered at the very thought of Il Serpente, a true family organization built on blood ties, because blood brokered loyalty. Blood was less likely to be bought.

Jovi was a part of this family, but not the way Carlo was. Because Jovi's father, the traitor Donatello, had betrayed his own brother—bringing dishonor to the family name and very nearly handing them all over to the authorities who stalked them.

This was a stain upon them all. Jovi alone of his father's family had been spared.

So he was *family*, yes. Blood where it counted. More importantly, he was a weapon.

The weapon, perhaps.

"Did you hear me?" Carlo's voice rose in pitch as he swung himself around the chair so he could look down at Jovi from the front. Allowing Jovi to watch, fascinated as always, as this big, powerful man who feared nothing and no one—a fact Carlo liked to broadcast whenever possible—looked more than a little *wary* at the sight of his supposedly lower-ranked cousin.

The way everyone did if they had the misfortune of seeing him.

Because there was rarely any reason to see Jovi that did not involve pain.

Carlo, as ever, could not hold Jovi's gaze. He looked away, and his shoulders hunched, more signs that he was intimidated by the cousin he liked to brag that *he* did not find frightening in the least.

He even spat on the ground, as if Jovi was a superstition in need of clearing. "You're a spooky *stronzo*," he muttered.

Jovi only waited. Carlo knew exactly why Jovi lived here. This was the home Jovi's father had inherited from his own father, as he had been the oldest D'Amato son in his generation. Donatello had been too soft for the family business, however, according to the stories everyone liked to tell. Jovi's grandfather had used to say that he had two heirs.

Donatello for the public family legacy, charming and academic and sophisticated. And the crafty, cunning, and wholly soulless Antonio for the family business, where sophistication was not required but brutality was celebrated.

Antonio had wanted nothing to do with this place after he had meted out bitter family justice upon Donatello, his wife, and his two young girls.

Jovi did not allow himself to think of them in other terms. His father and mother. His sisters.

They had all lost the right to those connections when Donatello betrayed their family.

He rarely permitted himself to think of them at all.

It was his cousin who seemed to enjoy bringing up ancient history whenever he came here, always pointing out the empty, echoing rooms. Always making certain to remind Jovi of the things he opted not to remember. Or, perhaps, reminding Jovi of his roots in the only way he could without risking Jovi's displeasure.

Despite what Carlo liked to tell the rest of Sicily, and

likely himself, both Jovi and Carlo knew very well that Carlo would never dare to *actually* insult his cousin. Here, in these private moments, Carlo's cowardice was always clear.

Carlo swallowed. Then took his time looking Jovi's way again. "Patri has a job for you," he said.

This, too, was obvious. Only a directive from Antonio himself could compel Carlo to visit this place of shame and despair, a stain upon the family name. There was no possibility that Carlo would ever come here to spend time with Jovi, to catch up or whatever it was people did when they had all of those social connections Jovi had never been permitted.

Even if Carlo wasn't terrified of Jovi, they would never connect in this way. Jovi shared blood with his family and their ancestors, here in Sicily and across the water in Calabria.

He did not share anything else.

That would require that he be made of something more than ice, and his uncle had made certain that he remained too cold to melt. Ever.

In truth, he preferred it that way.

Sometimes Jovi walked through the crowded squares of Palermo or drove past the beaches in summer. They were always teeming with people having their coffees and their harder drinks. Talking loudly, waving their hands in the air. Clustered together over tiny tables in public spaces or flung about in abandon on the sand, entirely unaware of their surroundings or what sort of monsters might be waiting there, watching.

Looking for a chance to strike.

He could not understand it.

Yet Jovi knew his cousin not only understood these things, but enjoyed them. Carlo maintained his never-ending stream of mistresses despite the carefully selected bride from a Calabrian family he'd married so ostentatiously in the cathedral in Palermo. Despite the vows Jovi had heard him make with his own duplicitous mouth. And the babies his dutiful wife, raised by men just like the one she married, had already provided him—three sons and counting.

Jovi did not make vows. He kept promises.

And he was not given to acts of sadism the way his cousin was.

He was Antonio's favorite form of detached and dispassionate justice, meted out in the face of betrayal, a broken word, or a disrespect too great to be ignored.

Or sometimes simply because Don Antonio felt like serving it to his enemies, with impunity.

Jovi was the final solution to problems that torturers and deviants like his cousin failed to solve.

Carlo knew as well as Jovi did that even Don Antonio took care to aim his best weapon carefully. What mattered was that Jovi was loyal. The son of a known traitor had to demonstrate his honor and devotion, without fail, forever. Even more so than the rest of the family. When he was young, Jovi had done what was asked of him—whatever was asked of him—because he'd had no choice if he wanted to live.

These days, everyone was aware that Don Antonio's orders to Jovi were a lot more polite than they had been. Or than they were to anyone else.

That was the trouble with crafting a perfect weapon.

There was always the worry that it could be aimed back at oneself.

Most of the time, Jovi simply waited, letting the ice in him grow thicker by the day, feeling nothing at all.

This was not to say that he was a saint or a monk. He fucked. A lot.

There was no shortage of women who were drawn to him as surely as reckless moths to an indifferent flame. He took what he was given, left them in pieces, and never took the time to learn their names or commit their faces to memory.

Sometimes, in the middle of the night, he would dream of the boy he barely remembered, a creature of heat and need, flesh and yearning. He dreamed of a bright, wild, intense boy who had delighted his father and made his mother laugh as she pretended to look to the heavens for the intercession of the saints.

But thinking of these things in the light of day was like telling himself fairy tales, anodyne little ditties about obedience, and Jovi could not relate to them. They were not the memories he allowed himself.

Because there was nothing in him that burned. He breathed destruction and delivered pain.

There was not one part of him that was not cold.

Even Carlo, who claimed he feared no man and was the scourge of many, was always wary in Jovi's presence.

Perhaps more than simply *wary*, Jovi thought.

Clearly disliking the quiet, Carlo outlined the situation that his father had sent him to share. It was no different from every other task Jovi had been set over the years. The particulars changed, but the outcome was always more or less the same. There were many men who played these games, who waged these wars in the dark shadows where fallen men created their empires, ripped down others, and were kings in all but name. There were many men who preened in their own power, little realizing that power, like any other commodity, could be bought and sold.

Because there was always more power. There was always someone more desperate to claim it. A circle without end.

These same men never understood that they as good as signed their own death warrants the moment they started throwing their weight around, because there were always higher bidders with deeper pockets. There were always new markets with more motivated sellers.

It was only a matter of time until they were all worth more dead than alive.

"We want him to hurt," Carlo said of the man in question today, some or other arms dealer in Eastern Europe. It didn't matter who he was, only that he'd decided he was more powerful than Il Serpente and could dictate his terms. "Eventually, he'll pay the price for his disrespect but first, a little pain."

Carlo carried himself as if he was a man of supreme beauty, though it was difficult to tell if his mistresses cared at all about his supposed good looks when his wallet was so well-upholstered and infinitely deep. He was not afraid to fight with his own hands—and, indeed, preferred it—a rarity at his level in an organization like theirs.

See again: sadist.

Accordingly, he kept himself in shape as if he anticipated that fight occurring at any time, despite his exalted position as his father's right-hand man.

It had been a long time since Jovi had heard his cousin complain to the rest of their cousins that it was difficult to keep up with his fitness when he was Sicilian, and there were too many delicacies forever on offer. Many a man had fallen into softness thanks to the preferred cuisine around the family tables and the local cafés, called bars.

The most dangerous men in the world are fat and round, Carlo had told Jovi once, his eyes dark with shame, when Jovi had effortlessly outperformed him in the gym.

Then they are not as dangerous as they think, Jovi had replied with his typical equanimity. *The men who fear them are the dangerous ones. The ones who do their bidding and could therefore do someone else's, too.*

Sometimes, like now, he thought his cousin remembered that conversation. There was something about the way Carlo refused to look at him sometimes that assured him it was something Carlo kept close. No doubt dreaming of the day that he would rule this family and give Jovi orders. Or better yet, get rid of Jovi altogether.

Jovi did not bother to inform his cousin that his loyalty was not transferable. He did not need to remind his cousin that his skills far outstripped Carlo's sick little games.

A day of reckoning would come, that was certain. These lessons could wait until then.

"Boris Ardelean is a collection of former Russian nationalities," Carlo told him in that sullen way of his, never quite able to look Jovi in the eye. "A mutt. A Czech national who should shut the fuck up, learn his place, and sell his guns. Instead…"

He shrugged. There were some who would see a shrug like that and lose control of their bowels. A shrug like that, from a man like him, had death written all over it.

Jovi was unaffected.

Carlo continued. "Instead, he thinks he can play games. He thinks he can dictate terms. He thinks he can go around the family to make his own name for himself. But… *Lu rispettu è misuratu, cu lu porta l'avi purtato.*"

"Respect is measured." Jovi agreed with the proverb his cousin was quoting. It was how they all lived. Or in Carlo's case, pretended he lived. "Whoever respects others will be respected in turn."

His cousin nodded. "Don Antonio likes his own name." The meaning was clear. This arms dealer needed a lesson. "Killing him would be too easy. How would he learn? How would he fully understand the depth of his disrespect?"

These were not questions that required an answer.

He stayed where he was, sitting still in his chair and watching as Carlo paced a little, as unable to stand still as he'd been when they'd both been small boys. Five and six and allowed to run wild while all the old women in black smiled at them and called them angels.

Only the fallen kind of angels, Jovi thought now. Fallen deep and hard, lost somewhere far beneath the surface of any lake of fire.

If he was an angel, it was the angel of death.

"This Boris has a daughter," Carlo was telling him. "He's been putting out feelers, seeing if he can marry her off in the old style to create an alliance. My father thinks Boris's only alliance should be with us."

Jovi inclined his head. "I understand."

For a moment, Carlo still stood there, staring down at Jovi, with that same wary look on his face that he often wore in his cousin's presence. To cover his uneasiness and fear, Jovi was certain.

"Other men might ask if she's pretty," Carlo pointed out. "If they might have a little fun, a little pleasure with their work. But not you."

"I do not believe in pleasure," Jovi replied. He didn't even bother to shrug. "In my work or anywhere else. It has no purpose."

Sex, killing—it was all the same to him. Women or men, it made no difference. Sometimes there was set dressing, the better to send a message. Sometimes mementos were required, whether before or after the death depended entirely on the reasons for the death.

He felt nothing about any of these things. He did his job.

Ice was ice wherever it was cold enough.

He could see that Carlo was holding back a sneer. That his cousin dearly wished he could speak frankly to him, though Carlo would never dare. Jovi even knew what he would say, as he'd said as much to others who had foolishly relayed it, imagining Jovi was the sort of man who would make alliances.

He's a freak, Carlo liked to tell the rest of the family. *Him and his freak father. If it was up to me, I never would have let him live.*

"I'm not the one who fears death, cousin," Jovi told

him now. "I don't have to dress it up and make it a game."

If he was anyone else, he thought Carlo would have lunged at him. He could see the loathing in his cousin's gaze. But then, of course, Carlo did nothing.

Because, at heart, he was a coward.

He showed this to Jovi every time they came face-to-face. Every single time.

And well did Carlo know it. Because he said nothing further. He only swallowed back whatever he wanted to say—no doubt thinking better of it and hating himself for it—and then turned around again to storm back into the house.

Jovi heard a crash from inside and assumed that Carlo was expressing his displeasure the way he often did, because he ran hot. And if asked, could claim any damage was an accident.

Jovi, obviously, had never asked.

Carlo was a coward, but he was also dangerous. He was sick in the way many men in their profession were sick. Pain was a game to them, not a means to an end—and because of this, they would be their own undoing.

It was written all over them.

It was what made Carlo who he was. His life was a preview of how he would die.

Jovi supposed his was, too. Ice unto ice, frozen into nothing.

This was as inevitable as the death of the daughter of a fool named Boris who thought he could play games with the likes of Antonio D'Amato.

Theirs was a world with very strict rules. They were

always the same rules. Death stalked them all, and none of them could escape it. None of them would.

Especially not if it came for them in the form of Jovi, Il Serpente's coldest flame.

He sat still for a while longer, until the sounds of his cousin faded away. Until the roar of Carlo's engine was swallowed up once more by the sunshine and the breeze. The careless birds wheeling overhead.

Only then did he rise and head into the villa filled with ghosts and the shattered remains of whatever glasses Carlo had thrown against the wall, so that Jovi could begin planning the most expedient way to do the thing he did best.

Because unlike his traitor of a father, when Jovi had promised his body, soul, and eternal loyalty to his uncle right here in this villa on the night of the great brotherly reckoning when Jovi had been eight years old—he'd meant it.

Copyright © 2025 Caitlin Crews

Did you fall in love with King's Heir of Hate?
Then you're sure to enjoy these other sensational stories by Caitlin Crews!

Kidnapped for His Revenge
Her Accidental Spanish Heir
Forbidden Greek Mistress
An Heir for Christmas
Sicilian Devil's Prisoner

Available now!

Get up to 4 Free Books!

We'll send you 2 free books from each series you try PLUS a free Mystery Gift.

FREE Value Over $25

Both the **Harlequin Presents** and **Harlequin Medical Romance** series feature exciting stories of passion and drama.

YES! Please send me 2 FREE novels from Harlequin Presents or Harlequin Medical Romance and my FREE gift (gift is worth about $10 retail). After receiving them, if I don't wish to receive any more books, I can return the shipping statement marked "cancel." If I don't cancel, I will receive 6 brand-new larger-print novels every month and be billed just $7.19 each in the U.S., or $7.99 each in Canada, or 4 brand-new Harlequin Medical Romance Larger-Print books every month and be billed just $7.19 each in the U.S. or $7.99 each in Canada, a savings of 20% off the cover price. It's quite a bargain! Shipping and handling is just 50¢ per book in the U.S. and $1.25 per book in Canada.* I understand that accepting the 2 free books and gift places me under no obligation to buy anything. I can always return a shipment and cancel at any time. The free books and gift are mine to keep no matter what I decide.

Choose one: ☐ **Harlequin Presents Larger-Print** (176/376 RPA G36Y)   ☐ **Harlequin Medical Romance** (171/371 BPA G36Y)   ☐ **Or Try Both!** (176/376 & 171/371 BPA G36Z)

Name (please print)

Address   Apt. #

City   State/Province   Zip/Postal Code

Email: Please check this box ☐ if you would like to receive newsletters and promotional emails from Harlequin Enterprises ULC and its affiliates. You can unsubscribe anytime.

Mail to the Harlequin Reader Service:
IN U.S.A.: P.O. Box 1341, Buffalo, NY 14240-8531
IN CANADA: P.O. Box 603, Fort Erie, Ontario L2A 5X3

Want to explore our other series or interested in ebooks? Visit www.ReaderService.com or call 1-800-873-8635.

---

*Terms and prices subject to change without notice. Prices do not include sales taxes, which will be charged (if applicable) based on your state or country of residence. Canadian residents will be charged applicable taxes. Offer not valid in Quebec. This offer is limited to one order per household. Books received may not be as shown. Not valid for current subscribers to the Harlequin Presents or Harlequin Medical Romance series. All orders subject to approval. Credit or debit balances in a customer's account(s) may be offset by any other outstanding balance owed by or to the customer. Please allow 4 to 6 weeks for delivery. Offer available while quantities last.

Your Privacy—Your information is being collected by Harlequin Enterprises ULC, operating as Harlequin Reader Service. For a complete summary of the information we collect, how we use this information and to whom it is disclosed, please visit our privacy notice located at https://corporate.harlequin.com/privacy-notice. Notice to California Residents – Under California law, you have specific rights to control and access your data. For more information on these rights and how to exercise them, visit https://corporate.harlequin.com/california-privacy. For additional information for residents of other U.S. states that provide their residents with certain rights with respect to personal data, visit https://corporate.harlequin.com/other-state-residents-privacy-rights/.

HPHM25